I0524704

A RINGSIDE
ROMANCE

MAKING IT
CHRISTINE D'ABO

RIPTIDE
PUBLISHING

Riptide Publishing
PO Box 1537
Burnsville, NC 28714
www.riptidepublishing.com

Making It

Cover art: L.C. Chase, lcchase.com/design.htm
Editors: Sarah Lyons, May Peterson, maypetersonbooks.com
Layout: L.C. Chase, lcchase.com/design.htm

ISBN: 978-1-62649-583-8

First edition
August, 2017

Also available in ebook:
ISBN: 978-1-62649-582-1

A RINGSIDE
ROMANCE

MAKING IT
CHRISTINE D'ABO

RIPTIDE
PUBLISHING

TABLE OF CONTENTS

Prologue 1
Chapter 1 9
Chapter 2 17
Chapter 3 27
Chapter 4 37
Chapter 5 45
Chapter 6 53
Chapter 7 61
Chapter 8 67
Chapter 9 77
Chapter 10 83
Chapter 11 95
Chapter 12 103
Chapter 13 117
Chapter 14 121
Chapter 15 127
Chapter 16 135
Chapter 17 141
Chapter 18 151
Chapter 19 159
Chapter 20 167
Chapter 21 175
Epilogue 181

PROLOGUE

Devan hated waiting. He'd never been particularly good at it, especially when it involved something important to him. If there was even the slightest chance that his dream could be snatched away, he'd barrel through until he made it a reality. Who cared if there was a mess left in his wake? That could be cleaned up, polished, and moved past.

His foster mom had tried to help overcome this particular personality quirk when he'd first come to live with them. She'd eventually given up.

He still hated waiting.

The PA system voice cut through the din of the emergency room. "Dr. Coi, code white. Dr. Coi, code white."

Devan turned the yellow hospital mask over and over in his hands, picking at the corners and snapping the elastic band. The only thing he hated more than waiting was feeling helpless. Sitting here, his mind turning over every worst-case scenario about what could happen to Meg and the baby . . . *fuck*.

Knowing if he and Eli were still going to be fathers was as high on his list of *important shit* as he could manage. It wasn't that he was simply nervous; that state of being was par for the course most days. Nervous would have been manageable. This was terror: scared raw, right through to his bones, chew him up and spit him out. Terror like he'd never felt from any fight he and Eli had ever had. What if it all fell apart, and they went home empty-handed again? What if something happened to Meg? He'd never be able to forgive himself.

Please, God, let Meg and the baby be okay.

Eli put a hand on his leg. "Put that on. If you don't, you know you're going to worry about getting the baby sick once you calm down enough to think about all the germs in here." They were the first words spoken between them since they'd arrived at the hospital. The first words since their latest argument and Meg's phone call. Eli's voice sounded wrong in Devan's ears, foreign.

"Right. Thanks." The elastic band felt odd around his ears and the air suddenly too close as he tried to calm down. He lasted about five minutes before he took it off again, earning him an eye roll from Eli.

Eli was like a rock beside him, but not the silently supportive kind. More like the actual hard, round kind that might start rolling in the opposite direction at any moment. It was startling to realize that although they were sitting together in the hospital, legs touching and waiting to hear if their baby would be okay, they were the furthest from each other emotionally as they'd ever been.

Their fights had grown more frequent in recent weeks. Devan had tried to figure out why one of them would eventually be set off. It was never anything big; money, the apartment, friends, that stuff they were solid on. It was the stupid little things.

Why's there no milk? *Fight.*

Where have you been? *Fight.*

Want to go to the movies? *Fight.*

Devan knew—regardless of what Meg thought—that having this baby was what they needed. It would not only be the glue to solidify the weak points of their relationship, but it would finally give him the last piece of his ideal life. Eli was a good husband, despite his occasional bad mood, and would make an excellent father as well. All they needed was for this baby to be born healthy, and everything would be fine.

With the memory of Meg's first miscarriage dancing in his head, Devan glanced at Eli. Rather than looking concerned, he appeared as though he was reviewing his training schedule. *Typical.*

"This is taking too long." Eli's voice was low, gravelly. "It can't be a good sign."

"It's probably just like the false alarm three weeks ago. Everything's fine." Devan spoke with a confidence he certainly didn't feel. The look on Eli's face said that he didn't buy it either.

Meg had been Devan's best friend growing up, and had offered to be their surrogate mother one night when the two of them had gotten into the tequila. She'd continued to make the offer sober, and after a bit of convincing, Devan had gotten Eli on board.

Now she was ten weeks pregnant and somewhere on the other side of the hospital wall with what sounded like another ectopic pregnancy.

It was probably nothing.

Devan turned the mask over in his hands again, before stopping to make tears in the paper.

"Will you stop fidgeting?" Eli glared at him. "That's not going to help."

"I'm not." The words snapped out of him. "Sorry." He set the mask on his lap for a moment before picking it up again. "There's no reason why it should be taking this long. The last time . . ." The remaining words evaporated in his mouth.

This wouldn't be like last time.

Eli grunted. "We'll know soon."

The clock on the wall told him they'd been *not knowing* for an hour and forty minutes now. What could they possibly be doing that it would take that long? Blood work maybe? An ultrasound?

Devan sighed. "I wish she would have let me come in."

"She probably didn't want to deal with your nerves." Eli reached over and took his hand. The contact should have been comforting. "It's going to be okay."

"What if it isn't?"

Eli squeezed his hand hard enough to make his fingers ache. "Then it isn't. There's nothing we can do."

Devan slowed his breathing and did his best to relax. He'd managed to get himself under control, when a nurse came through the automatic double doors. "Devan Walsh?"

He got to his feet so quickly that he yanked Eli's arm and the mask fluttered to the floor. "That's me."

"She'd like to see you." The nurse eyed Eli. "You're the husband?"

Eli nodded and stood.

"This way, please." She scanned her ID badge and the doors swung open. "They took her to maternity."

As they passed the little emergency room sick bays on their way to maternity, Devan tried to ignore the people within. Of course, he failed and caught glimpses of the patients. Elderly man surrounded by family, little kid and mom, woman and her husband. They kept going past the emergency room to the elevators. Up to the seventh floor, down the hall all the way to the last room. The nurse stopped and stuck her head around the drape before indicating they could go in.

"Oh hon, are you okay? You look so tired. Do you need anything?" Devan rushed to Meg's side, not liking how pale she looked. Her blue eyes were bloodshot, her black hair was stringy around her cheeks, and her body looked so small in the large bed.

Eli stood with his back to the drape. As always, he was quiet, observing, not getting involved the way Devan did. Not that Devan gave him much of a chance.

Meg had been crying, the tear tracks visible, but mostly dry. She reached over and took his hand. "I'll be fine."

Relief hit him far harder than he thought it would. "Thank God. I was getting really worried out there waiting for you. I mean, I wasn't even freaking out about the germs. No doubt I'll probably get out of here with three strains of the flu—"

"Devan, shut up." Eli's voice hitched, causing Devan to turn to look at him.

Meg squeezed his hand again. "It's okay. I've been his friend longer than you've been married. I know about the nervous rambling."

"Yeah, she knows me." He grinned before turning back to Meg. "If I weren't gay, we'd have been hitched ages ago."

Her smile was sad, but oh so very Meg. "We probably would have. Though you're a slob and would have driven me nuts."

"But this way I get the best of both worlds. I get you in my life, being the mother of my kid, and I get this bald, super-sexy fighter guy. Even if he's a bit rough around the edges." Even if they fought, and the chasm between them was spreading further apart.

Meg's smile wavered, morphing into a frown for a moment before tears slid down her cheeks once more. "I'm so sorry."

"Sorry for what?" Devan leaned over and kissed her forehead. "You're amazing."

She shook her head. "I . . . I lost the baby."

Devan continued to push her bangs from her sweaty forehead. He'd heard the words. They'd registered in his brain, coalescing there. But his body refused to do anything to acknowledge them. He continued to brush Meg's hair and wipe the tears from her face.

Meg reached up and took his hand in hers. "Say something. Please."

Right, this wasn't about him. This was Meg, his best friend and the mother of their . . . His throat began to tighten and tears welled up, causing him to blink.

Devan let out a sob. Only one. He then squeezed her hand. "You're okay, right? Were there complications? Did this cause any damage?"

"I'm okay. The doctor said this thing can happen. Does happen."

Did happen.

"Hon, it's okay." Devan kissed her knuckles. "Not your fault. Let us look after you for now."

"I'm willing to try again." She sat up a bit straighter. "Not like tomorrow or anything. But I'll go through the in vitro again. I want to do this for you. I want this *for* you."

"No."

They both looked at Eli, who appeared as though he'd been stabbed. Devan felt the shock of his words like a shot to the chest. "What do you mean, no?"

"Exactly what I said." His gaze locked on to Devan's, and there was no mistaking the finality of his resolve. "I won't go through this again. I can't." Without another word, he turned and walked away.

Meg shoved at his hands. "Go."

"But—"

"*Go.*"

Devan was moving before he realized it. Eli's long legs had put him far ahead already, forcing Devan into a near run to try to catch him. He finally pulled him to a stop outside the elevator. "Eli, wait."

His husband of six months stopped, keeping his back to him.

The doors slid open, letting five people out, drawing attention to the drama that was unfolding whether he wanted it to or not. Devan hesitated, but they needed to have this conversation sooner rather than later. "I know you're hurting too. We all are. Come here and let me hug you."

Eli didn't move. "I can't do this."

His nerves chose that moment to begin to misfire, creating the sensation of creeping ants below his skin. Devan didn't know exactly what Eli meant, not really. Eli was hurting and didn't know what he was saying. "I know the thought of going through this again is painful, especially after we just found out a few minutes ago about the . . . about the miscarriage. I think Meg's probably still in shock. We don't have to do the baby thing again for a while. It's best if we don't. We can wait a month, or maybe more, if that's what you need."

"I don't mean the baby."

Devan's stomach churned, making it difficult to think. "Okay. We can talk at home if you want."

"Devan—"

"I should probably go back and stay with Meg for a while though."

When Eli finally turned around, Devan was shocked to see tears. Eli never cried. He was the toughest man Devan had ever met. He'd seen him demolish opponents in the octagon, and verbally in the prefight interviews. Tears were for the weak. For Devan.

Devan swallowed hard. "Please don't. Whatever it is you're going to say, please . . . don't."

Eli didn't back down. He took a step closer, his wet face shining from the glow of the dim hospital light. "I can't do *us* anymore."

Bile rose, and Devan had to swallow it down hard. "What?" It barely came out as a whisper.

"You and I. Everything happened so fast. We weren't ready to get married, and definitely not ready for a family." He glanced over at an orderly, who was pushing an empty stretcher down the hall. "I'm on the cusp of making something happen with my career. I have a match next month that I'm nowhere near prepared for. We've been fighting when I should've been at the gym training. I've been planning for a baby that we're never going to have."

The pain in Eli's voice gave Devan a straw to grasp. "I know I've been hard to live with. I'll do better. We'll get better, and then we can still have a baby."

"That's what I'm trying to tell you. I don't want one."

"But . . ." Devan inched closer. "You said you did."

"I lied. *You* wanted to get married. *You* wanted a kid. I wanted you." Eli shook his head. "I'm going back to our place. I'll get my belongings and be gone before you get back. Thank Meg for me. Tell her I'm sorry. She went through a lot for us."

All for nothing. "Please don't do this."

Eli tossed the car keys to him as the elevator doors opened once more. "Keep the car. You'll need it more than I will."

Eli turned, hands in his pockets, and stepped into the elevator.

Devan could only watch as the doors slid shut, his body shaking as he clenched the car keys in his hand. The two most important people in his life were both hurting, each in a different way. Meg had given so much, and was still willing to give more despite what she'd been through physically and emotionally. Eli had simply left.

"Fuck you, then." He wiped the tears from his face and went back down the hall to Meg.

The nurse was checking her blood pressure when he finally stepped into the room. "She's doing really well. The doctor will be in to go over what to expect in the next few days."

"What?" He walked around to the other side of the bed. "I thought . . ."

"Remember? It . . . ah doesn't happen all at once." Meg couldn't meet his eyes. "It takes a few days."

"Right." His heart ached a bit more. "I'll take some time off work so you're not alone."

"You don't have to do that."

The nurse pulled the Velcro cuff from Meg's arm. "Let your man pamper you. Plus, it's good to have someone with you. As support."

Meg waited for the nurse to leave before she met his gaze. "Where's Eli?"

"He's gone."

"I knew this would be hard on you, but I didn't think *he'd* take it that hard."

It was weird how he'd gone from being overwhelmed by his emotions to feeling a bit dead inside. "I mean he's leaving me."

"What?" Meg bolted upright. "The hell he is. He loves you."

"Yeah, apparently not enough." He straightened his shoulders. "Well, fuck him. I have you and don't need anyone else."

"You needed this baby." Meg leaned back against the pillows, wincing. "It might have made a difference."

"I don't think it would have. He . . . Things haven't been great for a while. Maybe I saw things that really weren't there." Dating, the sex, their engagement, they had been a whirlwind. "I did want a family. Do want. I thought he did as well."

How had things gone so wrong, so fast? He loved Eli, loved the idea of the life they'd been building. But apparently even if you spent time polishing a turd, that didn't magically turn it into gold.

"I can't worry about Eli tonight."

Meg slid her hand across his. "I was serious. The doctor still has all the genetic material. We'll have to talk to him, try and figure out exactly what we need to do, but I'm willing to have your baby."

Was that something he could do alone?

Devan smiled at her. "Let's focus on getting you healthy. We'll figure the rest out later."

Even if that meant going it alone.

CHAPTER ONE

Three years later

Eli hadn't realized how badly he'd needed to come home. Toronto was a place like any other, a city that welcomed dreamers, that laid opportunity in front of its citizens and dared them to go for it. Toronto was a piece of him, the thing that had cemented the foundation of his self and allowed him to build up.

Strange, then, that he'd gone to such lengths to avoid coming back here.

A police car blasted by on the street behind him as he stood inside the front of Ringside Gym, staring. God, this place . . . so many memories, both good and bad, were tied here: bruises, tears, and hours of laughter. This little hole-in-the-wall gym had been at the heart of his teen years, had played a huge part in making him the man he was today.

He'd always known that Zack would eventually get this place up and running again—that man didn't know how to quit once he'd set his mind to something—but *this*? The new sign, announcing to the city that Ringside Gym was opened for business, shone bright in the daylight. Everything was beyond his expectations. He stepped further inside, letting the smell of sweat and the echo of voices wash over him.

The gym, while still holding on to some of the old features, was fresh and clean in a way that it hadn't been when he'd hung out here as a teen. The ring in the center of the room was original, that much was obvious from the chipped wood around the base and the dull color of the ropes. The place wasn't overly busy, though that wasn't surprising given the time of day. Two men were practicing punches by the side mirror, while a woman was using the heavy bag.

The city, this place, for a second, washed away the pain and loneliness of the last three years of his life. Seeing his childhood haven resurrected was worth the deluge of reminders of the life he'd walked away from all those years ago.

"Eli!"

One moment he was standing by the ring and the next he was being squeezed by a smiling Zack Anderson. He returned the hug, making sure to give Zack's arms a bit of a once-over. "Dude, you're wasting away. You're losing all of your muscle mass. I thought you said you were at this place twenty-four seven?" He wasn't that bad, but Eli hadn't pushed Zack's buttons in far too long.

"Do you honestly think I have time to do anything other than paperwork? I train a bit here and there when I have a chance." Zack pulled back, but kept his hand on Eli's shoulder. "Now I know why Russel was always on the hefty side."

"That had more to do with the beer and watching TV than being busy." Eli looked around, not sure what to take in first. "Dude, you've done an amazing job."

Eli couldn't help but notice the strain that had always characterized Zack's personality was gone. He was smiling, and his eyes sparkled in a wonderfully unfamiliar way. "You look good, man."

Zack grinned. "Let me give you the tour. I also have someone I want you to meet."

Ah, a guy. That makes sense.

They walked into the small office that once had held more boxes of old files than there'd been room for living people. The musty scent that used to permeate every corner of the place was gone, replaced with fresh paint fumes. The best improvement was the thin man sitting behind a small computer desk, glaring at the screen. His hair was a bit long, covering part of the left side of his face. There was an intelligence in his eyes that Eli couldn't help but notice.

"Hello, handsome." Eli wasn't normally one to flirt, but he couldn't help it, and chuckled when Zack stiffened beside him. "You come around here often?"

"Back off. I don't care what your MMA rank is, I'll kick your ass," Zack growled. "Nolan, this asshole is Eli McGovern. Eli, this is my partner, Nolan."

There was no missing the emphasis on the word *partner*. The memory of Devan's face flashed in his mind, and he immediately squashed it. Eli bumped Zack out of the way as he leaned over the desk and held out his hand to Nolan. "Nice to meet anyone who can tolerate Zack."

Nolan's smile was more cute than charming. "Thank you so much for coming to help us with the grand opening. Having you here is going to generate so much publicity for the gym, I'll have to setup a wait list for registration."

"I still can't believe you've managed to get everything going again, Zack." Eli turned to look through the office door, a wave of nostalgia washing over him. "It's perfect."

"Everything is up and running. You can practice here too." Zack grabbed his forearm and gave it a squeeze. "Don't want you softening up while you're on vacation."

It was weird to think of having any time off. Eli had been on the road, in the gym, or competing for nearly three years now. "The nursing home won't let me stay with Mom, so I'll have plenty of time to work out."

This was the second major stroke his mom had gone through in four years. As much as he hadn't wanted to come back home and risk reopening the festering wound that had replaced his failed marriage, he couldn't ignore his mom's deterioration and worsening dementia.

He was here for her, here for Ringside's opening, and that was all.

"It will be so amazing to have a well-known fighter here. Has Zack shown you the steam room?" Nolan got to his feet a bit too quickly and banged his knee. "Ouch."

"Not a lot of room in here." Zack moved around to help Nolan. The smile they shared was an unexpected stab to Eli's heart. "Nolan is also determined to get our yoga studio open. Can't leave well enough alone, this one."

The urge to run hit Eli. Jesus, Zack was happy and clearly in love. Because Eli'd screwed his marriage up didn't mean he couldn't be happy for his friend.

Focus on the here and now. Smarten up. "Yoga is great for core strength and it gives you a different way of getting people into the gym."

Nolan stopped moving, turned, and faced Eli. "I'm sorry, would you be so kind as to repeat that, please?"

Zack groaned. "Please don't."

"Oh no, he really needs to." Nolan's grin could have powered a small country for a year. "I believe your friend and *professional athlete* just said that I was right."

"Traitor." Zack spun Nolan around toward the back of the gym, but not before Eli caught the sparkle in his eyes. "This way."

For a heartbeat, Eli couldn't move.

His gaze had locked on to Zack's hand and how his thumb stroked the side of Nolan's neck as they walked away. It was a simple touch, casual in a way that betrayed their easy intimacy. Eli hadn't touched anyone like that for three years. His hands were built for destruction, not love.

Devan laughed as he threw Eli's dirty T-shirt at him. "I can't believe how disgusting your shit gets."

"The stink helps knock my opponents out." He tossed the shirt in the hamper before making his way to Devan.

"Don't touch me, you're gross." He didn't pull away when Eli wrapped his arms around him. "God, go shower."

Eli reached up and cupped Devan's cheek. "Why don't you come join me?"

There it was, the sparkle in his eyes that always sent blood to Eli's cock. Devan leaned in and placed a gentle kiss to his lips. "Sweet talker. Let's go."

"Dude, you coming?" Zack had turned back to face him.

He shoved memories of Devan deep down into the recesses of his brain and nodded. "Yeah. Show me this yoga space."

Over the next half hour, Zack and Nolan took him around the gym, while Eli and Zack reminisced. The scent of fresh paint and wood breathed life into his soul. If this rundown place could be resurrected, then there was hope for anything.

And everyone.

The yoga studio was nearly finished, still needing some of the mirrors to be placed on the wall.

"Should be done for the grand opening next week." Nolan leaned against Zack's side as they surveyed their accomplishment. "I wanted it to be a hot-yoga studio, but there was no way we could afford that yet."

Eli's head had started to pound, no doubt from the lack of sleep and the need to eat. He walked fully into the studio and did his best to ignore the quick kiss Zack planted on Nolan's cheek.

"Hot yoga is a big draw." Eli moved away from the leaning mirrors, his gaze now fixed on the exposed pipes in the ceiling. "It would be expensive to convert this place though."

"Maybe if we expand to a second location." Zack draped his arm around Nolan's shoulder as Eli turned to face them once more.

The pounding in Eli's head intensified. "I think I'm going to head back to Mom's. I need to lie down for a bit."

"Sure." Zack frowned in a way that told Eli he had a thousand questions but wasn't going to ask. "Need a drive?"

"Naw, I'll be good. I rented a car."

"Max wanted us to come by the bar tomorrow night for a private party." Zack reached into his pocket and pulled out a business card. "In case you forgot the address."

"Thanks. Not open on Mondays?"

"Nope, so it will only be the five of us."

Five? That meant Max had also found someone while Eli had been away. "I can't wait to see him."

"Before you go, I wanted to show you the promo." Nolan disappeared into the hallway before Eli had a chance to argue.

"He's very excited about the promo." Zack smirked. "Even if you don't like it, lie. It will make his day."

Eli didn't know what Zack was worried about. Nolan came back with several posters that featured the Ringside logo, the date of the grand opening, and Eli's professional headshot. "I hope you don't mind. I spoke with your manager, and he sent the picture. I figured if we're going to promote the fact that MMA-up-and-comer Eli McGovern is our guest of honor, then I wanted to do it right."

"It's pretty damn good. Can I take one?"

Nolan rolled the poster up and handed it over. "I've reached out to local media, bloggers, and the newspapers. We also have a special event for Big Brothers Big Sisters. I have a friend over there who said the kids can't wait to meet you."

This was a bigger event than Eli had assumed. Not that he minded: Big Brothers Big Sisters had been a godsend for him as a kid; it was the least he could do to give back. "Sounds good."

"You okay?" Zack squeezed his shoulder.

"I've been on the go too long today. I have some shit to do at Mom's place, then I'll probably crash."

"Yeah, sure." Zack leaned in and gave Nolan a kiss. "I'll walk him out."

"Sure. Nice to meet you."

Eli nodded and followed Zack down the stairs and out to the street and the city air. The moment he took a deep breath, some of the tension bled away. "I hadn't realized how hard it would be to come home."

Zack crossed his arms. "How's your mom doing?"

"I haven't seen her yet. The staff at the nursing home says she's not bad, considering how big this last stroke was."

"Shit. I'm sorry, man."

"Nearly three months of hell." And he wasn't there for her. Again. Despite knowing she was in a safe place, getting the best possible care, he'd grown too comfortable with the idea of someone else looking after her. "Doctor thinks she might show some more improvement, but it's hard to say at this point."

"That's something."

"My manager, Stephan, is pissed that I'm here, but I needed to make sure she's doing okay." He couldn't afford to fall off everyone's radar at this stage of his career, but this was his mom. It didn't matter that Stephan had been trying to get another fight lined up for him. If he walked into the cage with his head somewhere else, he'd get his ass handed to him. No, it was for the best that he was here, at least for now.

Eli loved to fight. He loved the camaraderie and grandstanding, and the blood, sweat, and tears. Devan used to caution him that one day all that would be over, and he'd need something to fall back on. That his family needed him to be there for them.

Devan . . .

He's not your concern anymore. You fucked that up.

He didn't have a family. The last time he'd spent any time with his mom, she'd had moments when she couldn't remember his name. The blank stare she'd leveled at him, the little shudder of fear when he'd reached out and taken her hand . . . Fuck, that was too much for him. And Devan?

Stephan had been thrilled when Eli told him he was unattached.

"Yeah, sure. I personally don't care about who you're fucking. I don't want to know. But let's just say there are some in your audience who wouldn't pay money to see you fight if they got a whiff of . . . certain things. So I'm going to tell you what I tell all my fighters: if you're gay, don't be."

He didn't need a family when he had a fast track to making it big in the ring. "Stephan will be after me to get back to Montreal as soon as I can. He hates the idea of me not being ready to fight at a moment's notice."

"He sounds like a real charmer." Zack shoved his hands in his pockets. "You seeing anyone?"

Eli forced his body to stay relaxed. "No. Why?"

"I was wondering if we should extend tomorrow's invitation to anyone else. Hate that you'll be flying solo."

"It's fine. I'm used to it." Fact of the matter was, he'd had no interest in dating for the past three years. He'd walked away from the best relationship he was likely to ever have; there was no sense putting another man through his shit.

"Are you going to call Devan?"

Eli's gaze snapped to Zack's. "I know it's been a while since we've hung out, but you know better than to go there."

Zack looked at him—hard—before he slowly nodded. "Wanted to see the state of things. I'll let you get to your mom's. And let me know if you need me to help with anything. She's family too."

"Thanks. She's good for now."

Zack backed away slowly. "We're here if you need us. See you tomorrow."

It was strange seeing Zack after all this time. Three years ago, when they'd last gotten together with Max, Zack had possessed as many edges and angles to his personality as Eli had. More. He wasn't going to chalk up Zack's softening to being in a relationship—he hadn't seen enough of Nolan to know for certain—but there was something churning in his stomach that told him that was the truth.

Would Eli have turned out the same if he'd stayed with Devan? Probably not. Zack's anger, his temper, had always been quick to boil over, but equally fast to dissipate. Experience and time could help with that.

Eli's issues were different.

Slipping into his rental car, Eli gave himself a moment to blank his mind. Emotions were too much of a liability both in the ring and in life.

Calm.

Focused.

Empty.

After letting out a slow breath, Eli pulled into traffic.

— CHAPTER — TWO

Devan frantically raced around his apartment, picking through the chaos in a vain attempt to find Mr. Fuzzy. There was no way Matthew would last five minutes at his sleepover with Aunt Meg if Mr. Fuzzy wasn't securely in his hands. Hell, he wouldn't make it out the door without screaming bloody blue murder.

"Where the hell are you?" He dropped to his knees and began to sort through the toys, the laundry he hadn't managed to put away, and the shredded remains of a *Maclean's* magazine he'd yet to read. He caught a flash of dark brown, and crawled across the floor. "Aha!" Mr. Fuzzy's floppy ear protruded from under the edge of the sofa. With a gentle tug, the well-loved bunny emerged, a wad of dust stuck to the chewed, stitched nose. It took a second to clean him off and check to ensure the white tail he'd made an attempt to sew back on was still safely attached. "You will live to flop another day."

Matthew's chatter echoed happily through the baby monitor. He'd rediscovered his truck this morning, which had given Devan a full thirty minutes of bliss. He should have done dishes, or rescued the laundry that had served as Matthew's playground last night before bed. Instead he'd sat staring at the monitor while sipping his coffee. One day, he promised himself that he'd learn to not feel guilty when he needed to relax.

No doubt that would be around the time Matthew was ready for college.

Only eighteen years to go!

Carefully checking the diaper bag once more, Devan went through the mental list of everything Meg would need for the next two days. It would be weird going about his Monday morning without having to prepare for daycare, but there was no way he'd be able to manage everything while getting a root canal.

Devan liked to think of himself as a superman, but dental work and painkillers sucked the life from him.

The buzzer went off, and he rushed to the panel. "Hey."

"It's Meg."

He buzzed her up and unlocked the front door before racing into Matthew's room. "Hey, big man. Auntie Meg's here. Want to go see Meg?'

Matthew was only eleven months old, but sometimes when he looked up at Devan, he swore his son understood so much more than the books said he should. Not to mention he had rich-brown eyes that reminded him so much of—

No. He wouldn't think that name.

"Hello?" Meg called out before groaning. "You're a slob."

"Let's go, buddy." With one easy swoop, he picked Matthew up, who giggled with glee. There might be moments when being a single dad was hard, but there were far more cases of it being the best job in the world. When he got back to the living room, Meg had already managed to pick up half the laundry, folding it into a quick pile. "Leave that. I'll get it when you're gone."

Meg took Matthew and smiled, though it didn't quite make it to her eyes. "There's my guy."

Matthew blew a raspberry in response.

"Hey, you okay? And don't try to bullshit me and say nothing." He knew Meg far too well for her to try to pull one over on him.

"I would never try to bullshit you, darling." The worry on her face bled away as she rubbed noses with Matthew. "I promise it's nothing serious. Nothing that will put a damper on me looking after my little man here."

"Think you'll ever wear Josh down about having a baby of your own?" No matter how much he'd tried to include her as the mom after she'd given birth to Matthew for him, Meg insisted that he was Devan's alone. She was content to be Aunt Meg and nothing more.

"Yeah, I don't think that will happen. Especially since we have this little guy to play with whenever the mood strikes us. I totally have the best of both worlds."

Handing over the diaper bag, Devan could tell there was still something bothering her. "So, what's going on?"

Meg sighed big and dramatically, but Devan knew she was serious to a degree. "I didn't want you to find out about this somewhere else." Shifting Matthew to her hip, she reached into the front pocket of her jeans and pulled out a folded piece of neon paper. "I debated telling you at all, but then I heard it on the radio and, well . . ."

It was strange how Devan knew that opening that paper was going to be the hardest thing he'd have to do. A sick burning formed in his stomach as he unfolded the sheet. The print was creased, distorting the letters and the address, making them difficult to read. Not that it mattered. The only thing he could stare at was the face looking up at him.

Eli.

"He's going to be at that gym doing some sort of demonstration. I don't know. But it's been on the sports news, and I got this at my gym. So, yeah. I thought you should hear it from a friend rather than it catch you off guard at work or something."

Matthew pulled on Meg's black hair and giggled.

How Devan had gone three years without seeing a picture of him was amazing. Toronto had gone a bit crazy for its native rising star, which meant Eli's image had become more visible. With a quick swipe of his thumb across Eli's face, Devan folded the paper. "Thanks."

"Are you okay?"

Sure, my ex is in town for the first time in three years and his name is going to be plastered all over the place. "Yeah. Why wouldn't I be?"

Meg snorted. "Maybe you can use this as a chance to get him to finally sign those divorce papers."

That had been the killer in how their relationship had ended. Eli had walked away from them, their marriage, their opportunity to have a family together—and, yet, he refused to sign the divorce papers Devan had sent him. If he'd cared so little about what they'd had, about what they'd wanted to have, then why wouldn't he finalize the divorce? Every time Devan had reach out to Eli's manager, Stephan, he was given another excuse why Eli couldn't talk to him.

"Sorry, he's training out of the country. I'll try and pass the message on."

"Sorry, he's in Calgary for a match. I can't distract him now."

"Sorry, you missed him."

"Sorry, he doesn't want to talk to you."

Eli would soon be the sorry one. This was Devan's opportunity to finally get out from under this cloud and move on with his life.

"Thanks. I'll check out this gym and see what I can learn about him being there. I'm sure he'll sign the papers."

"Well, if you need us to take Mattie here again, let me know." She adjusted both him and the bag. "Okay, my little man. Say bye to Daddy. He's going to be a big baby tomorrow at the dentist."

"Dude, it's a root canal! I think it's reasonable to be a baby."

Matthew looked between them, and held up his hand to scrunch his fingers into a small fist. "Ba ba."

"Bye, baby." Devan kissed him on the forehead, then blew a raspberry on his cheek. "Be a good boy for Aunt Meg and Uncle Josh."

When the door clicked closed behind them, Devan fell onto the couch and sat staring at the wall. Eli was in town. The man who'd made him the happiest he'd ever been, and the most miserable, was back in Toronto.

He'd done his best to push away the memories of their last night together, the final fight—God, it hadn't even been *that* much of a fight—that'd ended their marriage. He'd racked his brain the days and weeks after Eli had left, trying to figure out exactly what he'd done that had pushed his husband away.

Ex-husband.

Devan knew exactly where the divorce papers were. The manila envelope had been in the same spot for the last six months: in the top drawer of his desk sitting in the corner of the living room. He'd given up trying to get Eli to sign, but in his mind, it no longer mattered. Their relationship was over and done, despite Devan wishing it wasn't.

After all these years, he still spent too much precious time trying to pinpoint where he'd gone wrong, what else he should have done to keep their marriage afloat. But the truth was, Eli "I'm a tough guy MMA fighter" hadn't loved him the way Devan had. He'd never understood why they'd fought about dumb shit that shouldn't have mattered. Things had started off so perfect between them, it had ripped his heart out when their marriage crashed and burned.

Maybe Meg was right, and it was time for him to take matters into his own hands. He knew where Eli would be, and it was a public venue. That would make any meltdowns less likely.

Opening the flyer once more, Devan looked down at the poor facsimile of the man who he'd loved without question from the moment they'd met. It could have been the ink, or the picture itself, but Devan couldn't help but think Eli looked great. Happy, like he'd never regretted leaving for a minute.

Devan had done his best to ignore everything Eli since their breakup, but it had been damn difficult when his ex had become the next big thing in the fighting world. Devan had never understood what had driven Eli to get in the ring, to fight and yell, to want to hurt another person. That wasn't the man he'd come to know; that wasn't the Eli who would run his hands through Devan's hair when they were watching television on the couch. Wasn't the man who would make love to him for hours, or would play pranks on him, teasing Devan when he'd fallen for them yet again.

Closing his eyes, he leaned his head against the cushions. "Fuck, no. Not again."

Whatever they'd shared was over and done. Even if Eli had changed, there was no way Devan would ever be able to trust him. And the last thing he wanted was for Eli to find out about Matthew.

That would open up far too many questions that he didn't want to answer.

No, he would make a point of showing up at this grand opening, divorce papers in hand, and finally get a resolution to the entire mess. Then he and Matthew could get on with the rest of their lives.

Eli pulled into the staff parking lot for Frantic and parked beside the three cars that were there. He'd spent most of the day trying to relax, though he'd given up after an hour and started doing some work on the downstairs bathroom at his mom's house. It had taken longer than normal in the shower to get the dust and mold off his body and from beneath his fingernails. It had felt good to do something physical.

Max had called him at the house earlier in the day to tell him that the staff door would be unlocked and to come in that way. He'd also bitched him out for not stopping by the bar to say hi. Typical Max, couldn't resist getting a dig in.

He'd barely opened the door when the sound of music and voices reached him. It sounded like there was more than Zack, Max, and their partners there. Shit. The last thing he wanted to be was social, but there was no way he'd be able to walk away from his friends. He'd already done too much of that in his life, and it was starting to take its toll on him. Coming back to Toronto, to his mom and his friends, had only served to remind him of how badly he'd screwed up.

Coming back to the place where he'd ruined his marriage.

He'd managed to go most of the past three years without spending more than a few minutes a day thinking about Devan. Since Eli'd landed back in Toronto, Devan was constantly on his mind. He wasn't even certain Devan still lived in the city.

Fuck it. He'd burned that bridge, and there was nothing he could do to make things right. Closing the door with a bang, he walked toward the noise in the bar. The place was mostly empty, except for a group of about ten people hovering around the bar. They hadn't seen him standing in the dark hallway off to the side, and it gave him the chance to take everything in.

Max was behind the bar mixing some sort of drink in a shaker. A hot guy who looked vaguely familiar was sitting on the bar cross-legged beside him. Max kept glancing up at him, smiling in a way Eli had never seen him do before. Clearly whoever the hot dude was, Max was more than taken with him.

Zack and Nolan were sitting side by side on stools and drinking what looked to be beers. There wasn't any obvious physical contact, but it didn't take anything to see that they were utterly in love.

The rest of the people around the bar didn't look familiar. They were all relaxed and seemed to know one another. Maybe this wouldn't be too bad. He took another few steps into the bar, then Zack saw him.

"Eli! About time you got here." Zack was up and over to Eli before he could take another step. "Get over here and let me introduce you. You've met Nolan." Nolan gave him a little wave. "Jerk on the bar is

Grady, Max's boyfriend. This is Teddy, the bouncer here; Cameron, the assistant manager; Samantha and Moe are bartenders; and Candace here is the DJ. Everyone, the one, the only, the disgustingly fantastic Eli McGovern."

Max poured the drink he'd been shaking into a cup and handed it over to Nolan. "You, my friend, look like you need a beer."

"Hit me." He shouldn't be drinking, wouldn't be if he were currently competing. But it had been a long time since he'd spent any time with the two men he considered his closest friends. "But make sure it's the good stuff."

"I've got a new microbrew that I know you'll love. Opened a fresh keg for tonight."

Eli eased himself onto a stool on the other side of Nolan, and accepted the beer as the conversation started up around him. Grady winked at him. "So you're the famous fighter of the bunch. I would pay serious money to watch you kick Max's ass. And, for the record, you're better looking like this than all hot and sweaty in the cage."

Eli chuckled. "You're the first person to say so."

"Grady is a former reality star," Nolan said in a mock whisper loud enough to be heard by all. "He thinks he knows everything there is about fame and fortune."

Another look up and the light went on in Eli's brain. "You're Grady Barnes. From that celebrity house thing."

Grady held up his glass. "I love it when they recognize me."

"Don't feed his ego, Eli." Max took the glass from Grady's hand and filled it to the top with water. "It's big enough."

"That's what he tells me in bed too." Grady laughed when everyone groaned.

Nolan waited for the others to start talking again before leaning in a bit closer. "I hope this is okay. When I spoke with Zack after you left, I got the impression that you and two couples might be a bit awkward. I thought a few extra bodies would help."

There was something about Nolan, something about his manner that Eli instantly appreciated. "Thank you."

Nolan nodded. "I didn't know if you had anyone special yourself. Zack hadn't mentioned anyone and, despite what this might sound like, I'm not normally one to pry."

Eli nodded, a rush of emotions washing over him. "There was someone a long time ago. It didn't work out."

"I'm sorry." Nolan brushed his hand through his hair, revealing a faint scar on the side of his head. "Until I met Zack, it had been a long time since I'd been with anyone. That loneliness can hurt."

Nolan certainly was a perceptive man. "That it can."

"What are you two whispering about?" Zack threw his arm over Nolan's shoulder. "You can't have him, Eli. I've had to train him in my ways, and he's mine now."

Once again, Eli was surprised to see the edge that used to comprise Zack's personality had faded away. There was a gentleness in his teasing that Eli wouldn't have thought possible before.

"Please don't go." Memories of the hurt in Devan's voice from that night still haunted him. He could easily have been one of these happy couples, sitting around enjoying a few drinks. Devan would have loved Grady, but no doubt would go off with Nolan and have a long conversation about books or politics or something. He'd always been good in social situations, something Eli always struggled with.

"Naw, I wouldn't do that to him. He seems like a nice enough guy." Eli saluted Nolan with his beer before taking a drink. "I don't have time for a relationship. Too much time training and fighting to spend it looking for someone special."

Eli ignored the look that passed between Max and Zack. "So, what have you assholes been doing for the past few years?"

That was all it took for the stories to start. The longer the guys spoke, the more Eli let his mind drift to the past. The memories didn't hurt so much as they reawakened a part of himself that he'd long thought gone. Fighting at Ringside after school, letting his anger and frustration bleed from him with every punch. Horsing around with Zack and Max in the ring until Russel would chase them out. Coming home to find a social worker there, and how terrified he'd been when they said his mom had had a stroke and should be in a nursing home.

Seeing Devan for the first time at the blood drive, and being completely caught off guard by the sudden pounding of his heart. Looking into Devan's hazel eyes as he'd pushed the needle into his arm, had opened a spot in his heart.

His romance with Devan had been fast, wonderful; their marriage had filled a void in his life that he hadn't realized was there. Especially with the changes in his mom's personality since she'd gotten ill. If things had simply stayed the way they'd been those months leading up to their wedding, everything would have been fine. Stephan wouldn't have been on him to keep his relationship under wraps. His mom's sudden desire to want nothing to do with Eli wouldn't have hurt so badly. Devan's need for more and more from their relationship wouldn't have felt like a weight drowning him.

God, Devan.

He'd never admit it to anyone, but he'd started thinking more and more about him in recent months. Memories would hit him at the oddest times—grocery shopping, lifting weights, those few minutes before sleep washed over him. A part of him had always expected Devan to reach out to him once he'd left, fight for their relationship. The radio silence had only served to reinforce that he'd made the right decision, walking away when he had. Still, he couldn't help but crave those moments of normalcy in a life that was anything but.

His head began to throb harder.

"You okay?" Nolan whispered.

"A bit of a headache. I had a concussion back in August. I've gotten the all clear, but sometimes my body still likes to remind me that I'm human when I push myself too much." It had only been an hour, but he knew the pounding wouldn't get any better. "I'm going to call it a night."

Max stopped laughing at whatever Grady had said to him. "Really? You just got here."

"Past my bedtime." Eli stood, hoping his discomfort didn't show. "I'll see you all on Saturday at the grand opening."

Zack stood. "I'll walk you out." This was clearly becoming a habit of Zack's.

Thankfully, Zack waited until they reached the employee door before he pulled him in for a hug. "Come down to the gym sooner if you want. If you're up for it. You can do a little boxing."

"I might. I have a bunch of shit to do at Mom's place. And I need to get down to the nursing home to see her."

If Zack knew he was deflecting, he didn't say so. "Fine. I'll see you Saturday at ten."

"Thanks."

He got three steps away when Zack called out, "You know I saw Devan a few times after you left."

Eli froze, but refused to turn around. "Yeah?"

"Yes. He was devastated. And confused. I can't say that I blamed him either. You two were always so happy together. I couldn't figure out why you walked away from him." Zack cleared his throat. "Was it the baby?"

"No." That had been a part of it, but Eli didn't know if he had the words to express his emotions.

"He deserved better than what you did to him."

"Yes, he did." He looked over his shoulder at Zack. "That's why I left."

Without another word, he got in his car and went home to the darkness.

CHAPTER THREE

Devan couldn't believe the line of people winding down the sidewalk outside of Ringside Gym. All these people were here to see Eli? Sure, he knew Eli was a pretty big name in the MMA community, but he wasn't *that* big. Was he?

Maybe this wasn't such a good idea after all.

The manila envelope was under his jacket, secured by his armpit. This way it was out of sight and safe. He didn't want to risk anything happening to the pages, or worse, someone like Stephan taking them from him. Shit, he hadn't considered Eli's manager might be here. Given how much Stephan had stonewalled him before now, there'd be no way he'd be allowed anywhere near Eli now.

Shit, shit, shit. The line shuffled forward another few steps, marching him closer to a potential clusterfuck.

The wind had picked up, and November was starting to make its presence felt. Devan pulled his hat down and wished he'd remembered to bring gloves with him. The line was long enough that he'd be frozen by the time he got inside. At least his mouth wasn't hurting any longer from the root canal.

A group of twentysomethings ahead of him all had posters rolled up. From the snippets of conversations he overheard, they were hoping to get some pictures with Eli.

"Dude is a beast."

"I heard he's gay."

"Really? That . . . *Really*?"

"That's what the boards say. He's not, like, out or anything. Can you imagine the shit he'd take if everyone knew he was gay?"

"No way. I don't believe it."

"I don't care who he fucks as long as I can Snapchat this shit."

Devan shoved his hands in his pockets a bit farther. Shit, maybe this *really* wasn't a good idea. No matter how angry he'd been at Eli for leaving the way he had, the last thing he wanted was to do something to ruin his career. And if Stephan was to be believed, that was exactly what would happen if Devan got involved.

Yeah, he should go home. Meg and Josh had taken Matthew again, and that wasn't fair after they'd watched him on Monday. If Devan was smart, he would tell his lawyer that Eli was in town and they could get someone from the office to bring over the papers, and Devan wouldn't have to come face-to-face with the man who'd broken his heart.

The line shuffled forward again.

Surprisingly, he wasn't waiting long before he got close enough to the door that he could see inside. There were lots of people milling around, checking out the gym, trying on boxing gloves. Kids ran around the inside of the boxing ring, bouncing off the ropes and doing somersaults on the canvas. Seeing them playing made Devan's heart ache. He hoped he'd be able to do everything to give Matthew the life he deserved. Being a single parent was harder than he'd ever anticipated, even with Meg's help. It wasn't the challenges of keeping everything organized, juggling Matthew's needs with his work schedule, or the exhaustion at the end of the day. No, the thing he found the hardest was the never-ending litany of self-doubt that traipsed through his mind.

Am I being strict enough? Should I read to him more? Do I give in to this temper tantrum? How can I afford for him to go to college? Will I be enough for him?

Still, no matter how hard things could get, seeing Matthew's beautiful brown eyes first thing in the morning, hearing his giggle when Devan tickled him, and the late-night cuddles made everything worth it. He had the child he'd always wanted, the career he loved, and his tiny apartment was homey enough. The one element that was missing was a partner to share his joys with.

Devan moved forward again without really paying attention. It wasn't until someone cleared their throat that he realized he was at the door. Hoping he wasn't blushing, he looked over at the man standing at the door, wearing a Ringside Gym sweatshirt that was out of place on his frame. "Sorry. I was gawking."

"That's fine." He held out his hand. "Hi, I'm Nolan, the manager. Are you here for a tour of the gym, or are you in line to meet Eli?"

Devan's throat tightened. *Nope, can't do it.* "I'm here for a tour."

That must have been the right thing to say, because Nolan brightened up. "Excellent. If you want to go in to the left, Zack will be taking a group around in about ten minutes."

Before Devan's brain registered what Nolan had said, he was escorted inside, and the next person behind him moved up.

Zack had to be Zack Anderson, Eli's friend. God, he hadn't seen him since a month after Eli had left. He'd been curious but respectful about the breakup, and hadn't pushed Devan for too many answers. No wonder Eli had come back to town; if there was one person that he was eternally loyal to, it was Zack.

This was undoubtedly enemy territory.

There were about ten people hovering around the ring, while the line to get Eli's autograph wrapped around the right side of the gym. He must be sitting at a table, because Devan caught a glimpse of his bald head through the crowd of waiting people. Okay, he could stand here for a minute, then duck out before either Zack or Eli knew he was here. Then he'd go home, thank Meg for babysitting, and have a beer. Maybe watch the *Murdoch Mysteries* episode he'd recorded the other night.

"Devan?"

He spun around, and his gaze locked onto the tall and still very intimidating form of Zack. *Shit, shit, shit.* "Um, hi."

Zack looked over Devan's shoulder toward the line, before indicating the opposite direction. "Why don't you come with me and we can talk?"

Devan could have run, but there was something different in Zack's voice, something he'd never heard before. Like an obedient child, he trailed along behind him, thankful that they weren't moving anywhere close to where Eli was sitting.

When they stepped into a small hall that held public washrooms, Devan sighed. "Look, I'm not here to cause any trouble."

Zack crossed his arms. "I never said you were. But I am wondering why after three years you're showing up again."

"Why I'm . . . Yeah, I guess you'd take his side in this." Devan reached into his coat and pulled out the envelope. "I'm here because he never signed the divorce papers. I haven't seen him since he walked out on me the night of . . . that night. He left me and yet never officially ended the relationship. I've been stuck in limbo for three years. It needs to stop."

Zack's arms slipped to his sides. "I can't believe he did that."

"Well, I have the unsigned documents here to prove it. Since he's in town, I figured this was my chance to get this thing over and done with once and for all. I don't want to cause a scene, but he's ignored all of my emails and letters, and every time I called, his manager wouldn't let me talk to him. I honestly wouldn't have come here if I'd had any other option."

Zack reached out and squeezed Devan's shoulder. "I'm sorry. Max and I talked a lot about what had happened between the two of you. Neither of us really understood why he left. He never spoke to either of us about it, and it wasn't really any of my business. I didn't want to bother you."

His throat tightened. "That makes three of us. He never gave me an explanation, not really."

"You two need to talk. I'll pull him aside. I can take you to the office so you have some privacy, and you can get some resolution on this here and now."

Zack's kindness caught him off guard. The tears that had merely threatened to appear moments ago welled up in his eyes. "Thanks."

"Hey, it's the least I can do for you. You didn't deserve to be treated like this. Come on."

Zack marched out to where Eli was surrounded by fans, leaned over, and whispered in his ear. Devan could tell the second Zack said his name. Eli's wide-eyed gaze shot up and landed on him almost immediately.

All the air left Devan's lungs, and for a moment, he thought he would faint. How could he have forgotten about the intense way Eli could look at a person? The way the light would shine in his brown eyes. Eli got to his feet as a fan shook his hand.

Shit, this was finally going to happen. He would once and for all be free to go about his life, without Eli's specter hanging over him.

He should probably go to the office that Zack had indicated. This was something private and didn't need to be done in front of the crowd. But when Eli finally extricated himself from the people around him and made his way over, Devan couldn't move.

Eli stopped far enough away that anyone watching wouldn't think they'd had any prior connection. "Dev? You're here."

"I . . . Yes." He swallowed hard. The envelope was growing damp in his hand. "How's your mom?"

"Still in the nursing home. She's okay." Eli's gaze drifted to the envelope. "Why? Are you okay? Is there something wrong?"

"You know why." It wasn't because Devan was still in love with him. It had nothing to do with the heartache that had lessened but stubbornly refused to go away. "I'm not going to let you put me off any longer. I need you to sign the divorce papers."

Eli's face contorted into a mask of confusion. "'Any longer'? I haven't . . . Divorce papers?"

"Yes, divorce papers." Anger ignited inside his chest. "Don't look so shocked. I've been trying to get you to sign them for ages."

"I didn't know." The crowd behind them was growing restless— shouts, claps, and people calling out Eli's name. "I can't do this now."

"Yes, you can. It takes three fucking seconds to sign the papers. Look, I brought them. Here."

"There are too many people around."

"They'll think you're signing an autograph."

"Devan." He closed his eyes and let out a breath. "Later. I'll do this later, when we can sit and talk."

"It's already been three years. How much more time do you need?" His rage threatened to bubble through his calm façade. "I can't do this." He shoved the envelope at Eli, only to watch it fall to the floor when he wouldn't take it. "If you ever loved me, even a little, you'll sign those. I have to go."

"Devan, wait—"

He didn't. Ignoring the multitude of curious onlookers, he raced for the exit.

Nolan held the door open for him as he ran out. "Thanks for coming!"

Devan barely noticed his surroundings as he strode home.

Eli's back and head ached after sitting in the folding chair for over an hour. The line of people looked to be finally thinning out, meaning he'd only have to do ten more minutes or so of this and he could leave.

If he thought a match in the ring was hard, it had nothing on making sustained small talk with strangers when his heart wasn't in it. As he took the last few pictures and signed the final poster, he couldn't help but notice Zack hovering around the edges of the line, glaring at him. Eli had been on the receiving end of that look on more than a few occasions, and knew that Zack wasn't about to let his talk with Devan go undiscussed. He couldn't blame him.

Devan had wanted a divorce, had apparently been trying to talk to him for three years, and Eli hadn't known. How could he have been so stupid to think that Devan would be content to live in limbo, waiting for Eli to reach out to him? Of course he wouldn't. Had their positions been reversed, Eli would have chased Devan down and demanded for things to be finalized.

God, he'd been a fool, and Devan had paid the price.

It had been a shock to the system to see Devan after all this time. He was still the same, his brown hair that crazy in-between length that gave it a slight wave. Eli had loved running his fingers through the strands, teasing and pulling the locks straight to watch them curl again. His hazel eyes full of emotion, a clear picture of exactly what Devan was feeling. It had been one of the most amazing things when they'd been together, to see the inner workings of the man who'd captured his heart.

He'd been a complete asshole, and Devan hadn't done a thing to deserve that treatment.

When the last group left and Eli finally got to his feet to stretch, he caught Zack's gaze. "What's up your ass?"

"My office."

Shit, he hadn't been called into the office at Ringside since he was fifteen. He waved and nodded to a few guys in the ring as he passed by, but his attention was fixed on Zack. He knew when he was in for a fight, could see the change in Zack's posture, the way he carried himself. Eli might not be able to take a shot right now, but that didn't make him any less of a fighter.

Eli kicked the door closed and stood there, arms crossed as Zack took up a similar posture opposite him. "What the fuck is the matter with you?"

"You left this on the floor." Zack picked up an envelope from the desk and held it out for him. "I can't believe how much of an asshole you are."

"That's none of your business."

"It damn well is when someone who I considered a good friend is acting like a stranger. I can't believe you've been stringing him along for three years. Jesus, Eli."

"I . . ." There was no way he'd be able to say what was in his head without it coming out wrong. Eli leaned against the door, letting it hold his weight. "I didn't know about the papers."

A muscle in Zack's jaw jumped. "You didn't *know* or you didn't *want* to know? Not once in three years did you consider that your husband might want a divorce, a chance to start over after you walked away from him? That you owed it to him to give him closure?"

"I didn't . . ." He groaned and let his eyes close. "Stephan kept me so busy since I left Toronto, I simply rode that wave of ignorance."

It wasn't until he saw Devan standing there, envelope in hand, that Eli had finally realized why his heart had been aching for months, why the loneliness licked at his soul at the oddest of times.

He didn't want his marriage to be over.

"You have to take responsibility and open this." Zack tossed it to the floor at Eli's feet. "Or are you a coward?"

Zack was right. There was no fixing what he'd done to Devan in the past; it didn't matter that his self-indulgent ignorance had kept him emotionally safe for years. He needed to make this better now. He didn't deserve a second chance, and Devan deserved to be free from him. Reaching down, he snatched the packet and pulled out the documents inside.

Swallowing past the lump in his throat, he stared at Devan's name centered at the top of the page. "How did he look to you?"

"You saw him. Scared and tired and angry." Zack sat down on the edge of his desk. "What the hell happened to the two of you?"

That was apparently the question of the century. "It wasn't working."

"Bullshit. Right up until a few months before you left Toronto, I'd never seen you happier. Neither had Max."

Eli shrugged. "I was. And then I wasn't."

"Then you owe it to him to sign those papers so he can get on with his life. You can't live your life away from here, doing God knows what, while Devan is trapped."

"I know."

"Then make this right. You came back to Toronto to help me, but the gym will be fine. Devan won't be."

"Yeah. I know." He'd done everything in his power to block the memory of the devastation on Devan's face when they'd learned Meg lost the baby. Not that he hadn't had more than a few nightmares over the years, all prominently featuring Devan. "Think he went home?"

"I don't think he was going out for a night on the town."

The throbbing of his head was no match for the guilt swirling inside him. "I'll sign these and take them to his place."

Zack nodded. "Are you going to talk to him?"

"No. But I want to put them in his hands, look him in the eyes." Talking would only lead to heartache. Best to rip this particular bandage off and finally be done with it. "I'll text you later."

"You better."

A quick check online told him that Devan was still in their old apartment. He couldn't image why Devan would want to stay where they'd once lived together; Eli sure as hell wouldn't. The drive through Toronto traffic gave him an uncomfortable amount of time to replay how this reunion could possibly go. None of the scenarios ended particularly well for him.

As he turned onto the street he'd once known better than most, he was struck by waves of déjà vu. He and Devan walking half-drunk from the pub around the corner. Picking Devan up and throwing him over his shoulder so he wouldn't have to walk through the snow on the walkway. Kissing Devan in the elevator on their way upstairs.

By the time he pulled the car into a visitor's parking spot, Eli didn't think he could go in. More than a few of his opponents would have laughed at the idea that Eli McGovern was scared of anything, let alone facing a man who was a fraction of his size. But what they didn't know was how deadly Devan could be with a few perfectly chosen words. Not that Eli had ever been on the receiving end of Devan's wit, but that didn't mean he wanted to be.

Come on, dude. You can take a punch and keep going.

Grabbing the envelope and a pen, Eli got out of the car and went inside before he could talk himself out of this. Luck was on his side when he got to the security door. Someone hadn't fully closed it, giving him access. It was better than having to buzz up.

The building had never been fancy, but the walls were rougher than he remembered. There was a smell in the air that couldn't be healthy. Why the hell was Devan still in this building? Surely, he could afford better?

He stood in front of the door that led to the place he'd once called home. The apartment number was the same, though the door had been painted green at some point. Closing his eyes, he took a breath and knocked.

From the other side of the door: "Just a second."

Eli should have stepped back, but he didn't want to give Devan the chance to slam the door in his face. The rush of adrenaline he normally got before a match surged through him. He knocked again.

"Coming."

Devan jerked the door open, his brown curly hair messy, his cheeks flushed and his hazel eyes sparkling as though he'd been laughing. Their eyes met, and Eli saw Devan's shock as strong as his own.

"You're here." Devan was clearly confused.

But not as much as he was. Because in Devan's arms was a small child who looked remarkably like Eli.

═ CHAPTER ═ FOUR

Devan couldn't breathe. Matthew was tugging at his earlobe and sucking his thumb. He'd been fussy since Devan got home. Teething most likely. He couldn't be sure if Matthew was in pain again, or if he'd picked up on Devan's shock and anger, but he began to cry.

Juggling his son to the other hip, he glared at Eli. "Why are you here?"

Eli held up the envelope in response. "You have a kid."

Devan had dreamed of this moment for years. His fantasies ranged from Eli coming home and begging Devan to take him back, to Eli coming home only to throw divorce papers at him. He'd not been prepared for Eli to *ever* know about Matthew. "Have you signed them?"

"We need to talk." Eli crossed his arms. "Are you going to invite me in?"

He could say no, and he knew Eli wouldn't do anything to force his way. He *should* say no and make Eli hand the papers over before leaving. Nothing good would come of Eli being back in this place and around his son.

It was the sound of Matthew's cooing that convinced him. "Ten minutes."

He turned his back on Eli and brought Matthew over to his playpen. "Da da da."

"Yes, baby, I'm here. You play with Mr. Fuzzy." He handed the bunny over, which immediately went into Matthew's mouth.

When he turned around, Eli had shut the door and taken his shoes off. "The place hasn't changed much."

"I happened to love how my apartment looked. I had so much more space after you left and could decorate how I liked, it was awesome." It was a complete lie. He'd painted the spare room to turn it into Matthew's nursery, but that had been the extent of the changes.

Eli walked up to the couch and tapped his finger on the top of the cushion. "I thought you wanted to replace this?"

"It's comfortable. Did you sign the papers?"

"No." Eli tossed the envelope on the couch. "You went and did it. You have a kid."

"I did and I do." Christ, this was a conversation that he'd been playing over and over in his head during nightmares. His guilt that never let him fully relax and enjoy the life that he'd worked so hard to build. But now that Eli was here, Devan knew he had to come clean. The anger bled from him as the tension tightened in his chest. "There's something I need to tell you about him."

The muscle in Eli's jaw jumped. "What's that?"

Devan closed his eyes momentarily. "There's a chance that he's yours."

The color drained from Eli's face. "*What*?"

God, he'd never thought in a million years that he'd ever have to make this confession, to give Eli a reason to stay around any longer than he needed to. Unfortunately, the truth wouldn't allow for that. Despite what Eli had done to him, how he'd crushed his heart, Devan couldn't keep this secret any longer.

Eli grabbed the back of the couch with both hands and leaned forward. "What do you mean there's a chance he's mine?"

"Exactly that." He wanted to sit on the couch, to sink so far into the cushions that he'd be hidden. This truth had been weighing on him for over a year, and now that the time had arrived to confess the truth, Devan wasn't sure exactly what to say.

Eli might have been in the wrong for not finalizing the divorce, but Devan was no better by withholding the truth about Matthew. "When I decided that I wanted to go forward and try again for a child, I gave the doctors a fresh sample." He'd been so nervous about being a single dad, about Meg having another miscarriage, but the chance to have a family of his own was worth the risk.

"But?" Eli's grip on the back of the couch hadn't relaxed.

"The doctor called me in shortly after we realized Meg was pregnant. Apparently, there'd been a mix-up at the lab. They used our original combined samples instead of the new one I'd provided." He'd never told Meg that. To this day, as far as she was concerned, the baby was all Devan's. "I was told that if we wanted to end the pregnancy, they would make the arrangements. But I couldn't do that. I'm sorry."

"Why weren't my samples destroyed?"

"I don't know. It was too late to do anything about it at that point. Meg was pregnant."

Eli's face had gone from white to red and his fists were balled at his sides. He was furious, despite his voice not being louder than normal. "When I'd walked out on you and made it perfectly clear that I didn't want a kid."

"I know that. It's not like I set out to screw you over. There'd been a mistake, one I had no control over. After all she'd gone through with the miscarriages, I wasn't about to ask her to have an abortion." God, the thought of it made him ill. "She was sacrificing her body for me again. This was the last time I was going to ask her to try. There was a chance he was mine, and that's all I needed."

"Jesus, Devan. Why didn't you tell me?"

A surprised laugh escaped him. "How? I couldn't get you to answer me about signing the divorce papers, and this wasn't exactly a conversation I wanted to pass through your manager." He could imagine Stephan's reaction to that little revelation. "Would it have made a difference? If it had turned out that he was yours, would you have miraculously changed your mind about wanting a family? Wanting to be with me? You would have hated me more than you do now, for forcing your hand."

"I don't hate you. I never did." Eli relaxed his grip as his gaze slid to Matthew. "You said that there's a chance that he's mine?"

"I don't know for certain. I never bothered getting a paternity test done. As far as I'm concerned, he's mine and you are my ex-husband." Or would be the moment he signed those papers. "I'm not sure why you came here. You could have signed the papers and mailed them."

Eli hadn't looked away from Matthew. "I wanted to look you in the eye when I apologized. I hadn't known about the divorce papers and wanted to explain. I'm glad that I did." He moved away from the couch and over to the playpen. Crouching down, he pressed his fingers against the mesh side. Matthew reached out and gave one of his fingers a squeeze, laughing when Eli wiggled them. "Would you have ever told me?"

"It was my decision to have a child, not yours. When you left . . ." Devan didn't know whether to laugh or cry. "When you left, I had a lot of time to think. Meg needed time as well. The miscarriage was really hard on her, despite not wanting the baby for herself. We talked a lot, but when she said she was willing to try one more time, I knew that this was what I really wanted. What I needed for *me*. Surprisingly, it had nothing whatsoever to do with you."

His birth family had been nonexistent. Vague memories of his biological mother would haunt him every now and again, but he couldn't trust that they were real. He was a child of the foster system. While he'd had the benefit of landing with a good family, that never lessened the pain he'd felt after being discarded by his biological mother.

No, he'd wanted someone to love and be loved by unconditionally. He thought he'd found that with Eli, and adding a child was simply sweetening the pot.

Too bad that hadn't worked out.

Eli smiled at Matthew before slowly getting to his feet. God, he was more attractive than when he'd left. Which was so not the thought Devan wanted to be having right now. He needed Eli to sign the papers and go. Devan needed for him to be gone once and for all so he could focus on what was important—his son.

Moving around to where the papers were, he picked up the envelope. "Let me get you a pen."

"How about you give me something else?"

Devan stopped in his tracks, having no idea where this was going. "What could I possibly want to give you?"

"A chance to apologize properly." Eli's gaze shifted from Matthew to the envelope in Devan's hands. "I'll sign them. I owe you that much. But I need to know what happened, why I didn't hear about this."

"Because your manager is an asshole."

Eli tensed. "If he's done this, kept you from me, then I need to know the details. My contract with him is . . . stiff. I can't confront him without knowing everything. He can ruin my career otherwise."

"That's not my problem." As Devan spoke, the words rang hollow. Eli might have hurt him, but standing here looking at him, Devan knew he didn't have it in himself to reciprocate.

Eli nodded, appearing defeated. "I know. I'm sorry."

Those were the words Devan had longed to hear for years now. Shit, he'd dreamed about it. Why couldn't he have come back on his own? "You asked me if I would have ever told you. Would you have listened if I had? I know you, know how that brain of yours works. You'd have gotten a call or email from me about Matthew, and you would have blamed me. 'Oh, there goes Devan again, trying to force me into something that I'm not ready for.'" Anger filled him, giving him courage he didn't normally feel. Devan moved until he was right in Eli's space. "If I hadn't come to the gym and talked to Zack, would you have come to see me?"

Devan was close enough he could see the emotions flit across Eli's face. When Eli swallowed, his gaze moved to watch the bob of Eli's Adam's apple. He should have been surprised when Eli reached out and gently circled the wrist of his hand that held the envelope, but he wasn't. He knew this man, almost as well as he knew himself. It hadn't been Eli's physical prowess that had initially attracted him—though that hadn't hurt—but rather his quiet kindness.

As Eli lifted Devan's hand up, the weight of the envelope nearly became too much. This had been an unwanted wedge between them for a long time now. It needed to be removed. Eli must have had the same thought. Taking the envelope from Devan, Eli moved in closer. "I fucked up with you."

"Yes, you did." Understatement of the goddamned century.

"Come out to supper with me." When Devan stiffened, Eli shifted his grip so he held Devan's hand. "We'll talk and I'll sign the papers."

"When?"

"I'm in Toronto for a month, maybe a bit longer depending on . . . well it doesn't matter. I'm here. I want to have a paternity test. I want to know if Matthew's mine."

"You said yourself you never wanted kids. What does it matter if he's biologically yours or not? I'm not asking you for any support or money. I don't want you to be this person who drifts in and out of his life." *In and out of* my *life.*

Eli stepped closer, so their mouths were only a few inches apart. "You have a child. A boy who might be mine. I can't walk away from this. Not without knowing."

"I should say no." Devan swallowed. He didn't know if he wanted to kiss Eli or cry.

"You don't owe me anything, I know that. But I think I have the right to know if I'm his father. I can't believe *you* don't want to have the truth." There was a sadness reflected in Eli's gaze, but Devan knew he would do exactly what Eli said. "Please."

God, he was a fool for considering this. Eli had not simply broken his heart, he'd shattered it. That wasn't something that they could recover from. Not easily at any rate. If Matthew turned out to be Eli's, Devan didn't know what he'd do with that information. He wouldn't love his son any less, but would Eli then suddenly want to be a part of their family? Would Devan let him?

Regardless, Eli was right about one thing. He did have the right to know if Matthew was his. "I'll consider getting a paternity testing kit. I just . . . Give me some time."

Eli nodded, his gaze back on Matthew. "Okay. Thank you."

"What if he's yours?" God, this was so screwed up. "What will you do?"

"I'm not going to take him from you if that's what you're worried about."

"I'm not." Shit, he hadn't considered that. "I . . ."

Eli gave Devan's hand a squeeze. "I'm not going to take your son from you. I . . . Can you imagine what kind of crap father I'd be? That's why I never wanted kids to begin with. I barely know how to look after myself."

Devan had always thought Eli would have made an amazing father. "Just because you didn't have a dad doesn't mean you'd make a bad one."

"We'll have to agree to disagree on that."

Another old argument Devan wasn't willing to rehash. "I'll look into what we have to do for a paternity test."

Eli nodded. "Thank you."

They stood there staring at one another as Matthew gurgled away. Normally always one to have a quip or comment, for the life of him, Devan didn't know what to say.

Eli rubbed his nose and cleared his throat. "So, about supper?"

"I can write everything down—"

"Devan. Please?" There was no arguing with that tone. "Do you still work at the clinic on King?"

Devan had been a phlebotomist for Canadian Blood Services for years. It was strangely the only thing he'd ever wanted to do with his life. "Yeah, still there."

"Are you working Wednesday night?"

"No." Devan's hands were clammy and shaking. He pulled from Eli's grasp, turning to look at Matthew, who'd fallen asleep in his playpen.

"I'll pick you up at the clinic. Take you out to supper, sign the papers, and we can talk about what Stephan did."

"And if I don't like how our dinner is going?"

"Leave. You don't need to make up an excuse. You can get up from the table, and I won't stop you."

This is such a horrible idea. "Fine. One meal. And this is not a date."

"Of course not. I'll pick you up Wednesday after work."

"I'll have to see if my sitter can stay longer first." And continuing with his newly acquired trend of acting on his bad ideas, he grabbed a crayon and a piece of paper from the floor and jotted down his cell number. "Text me tomorrow and I'll let you know for certain."

Eli hesitated, but gently took the paper from him. "Thank you."

"You better go. I need to get him cleaned up and into bed."

Eli nodded. "What's his name?"

"Matthew James."

"That's nice." Eli's gaze seemed to get stuck on Matthew. He shook his head before moving toward the door. "I'll text you around noon."

"Yup." Why was he doing this? Nothing positive could come from it. Nothing at all.

Eli slipped on his shoes and opened the door. "I'll talk to you tomorrow."

The moment the door closed, Devan raced across his small apartment and flicked the lock. Then, for good measure, he fastened the security chain in place as well. Neither of those would keep him safe from the attack of emotions he was currently suffering.

Heart racing and body shaking, Devan was terrified he'd drop Matthew, but the need to touch and hold his baby was too strong to ignore. Picking him up from the playpen, he relaxed as Matthew snuggled in, pressing his face to the side of Devan's throat before resuming his thumb-sucking. The scent of the baby shampoo was still fresh from his bath last night, and Devan pressed his nose to Matthew's head to breath it in.

Everything would be fine.

This thing with Eli was only a bump in the road. He'd chosen to walk away, been perfectly clear that this wasn't the life he'd wanted. One dinner wasn't going to change that. No, they'd have their dinner. Devan would give it the whole meal, enjoy a nice glass of wine and an expensive dessert, and then he'd make Eli sign the papers.

For now, he'd take Matthew, lie down, and have a good long cuddle.

CHAPTER FIVE

Eli hadn't slept at all last night. After he'd gotten back to his mom's house, he'd grabbed a bottle of water and stretched out on his bed, only to stare at a crack in the ceiling plaster. He'd been in the house for nearly a week now, and he'd not noticed the split and peeled plaster before then. It shouldn't have bothered him—the house was old and there were no doubt more cracks that hadn't caught his attention—but there was something about this one that pissed him off.

It had been there, right above him this whole time, and he hadn't noticed.

That was apparently a theme of his life that he hadn't been aware of until recently. So the damn crack and his conscience kept him up for hours. Three years ago, he'd been a mess: angry at the world and depressed. Between trying to help his mom and going through the miscarriages with Meg, Eli's emotional reserves had been depleted. Not that he'd said anything to anyone. That wasn't how a man was supposed to be. He'd pushed himself on and on until he was little more than a shell. Meg's last miscarriage had taken the final drop of feeling from him, leaving him numb.

The night he'd left Devan at the hospital, he'd called Stephan looking for help; the call was a shock to them both. Like always, Stephan had made everything seem so easy. *"Come to Montreal and work out here. Take the time you need to focus on your career and everything else will slot into place."* And it had worked for a while. He'd become a one-man machine, pushing his body to extremes until that empty shell was encased in impenetrable muscle and sinew. Nothing was getting in or out. Eli continued on once again.

But like the unseen crack in the ceiling, his life had been split, and he hadn't noticed the wound. Not until Devan had opened the door and he'd come face-to-face with Matthew.

This morning, he'd gone to the hardware store and gotten what he needed to patch the crack. It helped to get his blood pumping, to clear his head, giving him the opportunity to think.

Devan had a child, one that might actually be *his*.

If the thought of being a father three years ago had scared him, seeing that beautiful boy had been downright terrifying. How could something so small, so damn near perfect, have come from him? It didn't seem possible. And, yet, the way he looked was so much like the pictures of himself as a child, they wouldn't have been out of place on the mantel downstairs.

Matthew *had* to be his.

Brown hair, rich-brown eyes: truly, Matthew could be biologically either of theirs. Devan's eyes were hazel, but he vaguely remembered something from high school biology about hazel being pretty much brown, and wasn't that a dominant trait? He couldn't quite remember. So Matthew could still be Devan's. Matthew's little nose was pudgy, like Devan's, but also looked a lot like Eli's mother's. God, there was no way to know for certain without a paternity test.

Slopping another gob of crack fill onto the plaster, Eli's emotions rolled from awe to anger. Devan had a child and wanted a divorce. Had Stephan not gotten in the way, Eli would have known, and maybe things would have been different. Maybe he would have come back to Toronto, begged Devan for forgiveness. Once upon a time, he'd had dreams about doing that very thing. But the longer he'd stayed out of Toronto, the harder it'd been to figure out a way to come home and make his relationship with Devan right again.

A glob of crack fill fell onto the drop cloth he'd spread on the mattress, dragging a growl from him. He'd done basic construction for years; a little home repair shouldn't present this much of a challenge. His mom's tenants hadn't been particularly rough on the building, but they hadn't taken great care either. Not surprising, given the age of the place. The electrical, the appliances, and especially the paint on the walls were past their prime and needed to be updated. He needed to, bit by bit, cover up and replace the memories of his childhood home.

It would give Eli something to do while he waited to text Devan.

His cell phone rang as another glob of crack fill fell to the drop cloth. He fished it out of his back pocket and tucked it under his chin. "Hello?"

"Are you ready to come back yet?" Stephan's voice crackled through the line. "Because this little vacation of yours is a pain in my ass."

Rage that was normally reserved for the ring flashed through him. "You asshole."

"Nice to see that you haven't resolved your anger issues while you were away."

"I saw Devan."

"Ah." Instead of the fear Eli had expected to hear from his manager, all he got was a sigh. "I'm not going to apologize for what I did."

"You kept him from me." *Kept me from knowing that I might have a son.*

"No, I kept you from destroying your career. Can you imagine what the press would have done had they found out you were having issues with a man? Someone you were romantically involved with? You wouldn't be in a position to complain, because you'd have had no career and I would have dropped your ass three years ago."

"You had no right—"

"I had every right." Stephan's voice felt like a gun blast in his ear. "I invested in you. And I was protecting that investment."

Eli swallowed hard, any response stuck tight in his throat.

"Now, if you're done having your little temper tantrum, I need to know the status of your vacation."

He shouldn't have felt guilty for needing to take time to be with his mom, but Stephan apparently knew which buttons to hit. "I'm stopping by the nursing home later today to check on Mom. The doctor said she's still not in great shape for visitors, but I'm going."

"So you're not planning on leaving Toronto anytime soon. Good." *Shit.* "Why?"

"Caulfield's team wants another run at you."

"No way." God, the dude got one lucky shot off and he thought he was king of the world. "Why the hell would I agree?"

"The ratings were some of the highest they've seen for a non-title fight. It's good PR for everyone."

Caulfield was notorious for being a dirty fighter. The crowds loved everything he did and the drama that he brought to the match. Eli wasn't as flashy, which brought about his own following, the people who loved his deadly precision. He didn't need the flash when he had the substance.

Eli got down from the bed and dropped the trowel to the floor. "You know how I felt about the last fight. No fucking way I'm getting in the cage with him again."

Stephan sighed. "Yeah, that's not going to work. See, when the organization found out you were in Toronto, they gave me a call. Seems they have another hurt fighter who was supposed to fight Caulfield on December tenth at the Air Canada Centre. It's not the main card, but pretty damn close. You'll be at the top of the undercard round."

It was obvious what Stephan was saying—sick mother or no, this was too good an opportunity to pass up. "I haven't seriously trained in months."

"Come on, I know you. You'll be fine." Stephan chuckled. "I don't *need* you to agree, but I don't like to overrule you. Say yes so I can pull the trigger on this. The money and exposure are exactly what you need. You know I wouldn't push you into this if I didn't think the risk was worth the reward. It's huge. Your chance to not only move up the ladder, but really get noticed by some important people."

If there was a way he could go back and talk his younger self out of signing with Stephan, he absolutely would. While Stephan had done wonders for his career, while Stephan had been there for Eli when life felt insurmountable, there were equally too many times when Stephan had forced his hand. *Fuck it.* It was only one fight, he would still be in Toronto for his mom and Devan if they needed him. "Make the call."

"You're a fucking rock star. I'll fill you in on the details when I get them. Three weeks, dude. Get ready."

By the time Stephan hung up, Eli had lost all desire to do any more work. God, he would need to start training now if he wasn't going to get himself killed. He could use Ringside for training, stay close, and possibly bring some fans in to help raise the gym's visibility.

Maybe Devan and Matthew would come watch.

He thumbed the screen of his phone, bringing it back to life. With a quick swipe, he brought up Devan's number. What he wouldn't give to call him, hear his voice for a few seconds. That would be going against their agreement, and if he wanted any chance of things to work out, then Eli knew he had to play by the rules. Pressing the text option, he typed a quick message.

It's me. How is tomorrow night looking?

If Devan was with a patient, then his response could be a few minutes. He remembered getting annoyed when they'd first started dating. They'd be in the middle of a text conversation, Eli would ask him a question, and then nothing. Devan would always laugh after. *"What, do you want my phone to be covered in blood? Gross."* Given how Eli felt about blood, it wasn't something he ever wanted to see outside of a match.

Eli went to the kitchen and made himself a protein shake. He'd nearly finished it when his phone buzzed.

My sitter said she can keep M for an extra few hours. I'll need to be home by seven.

For the first time in what felt like an eternity, Eli smiled.

I'll pick you up at 5:30. Supper @ 6.

Shit, he was actually going to do this. Which meant he needed to book a reservation somewhere. Devan had always been the one to manage their dinner arrangements when they'd been together. He'd need to get some help if he didn't want to screw this up. There was one person he knew could help him out. Dialing Ringside, he fiddled with his glass as he waited for an answer.

"Ringside Gym. Nolan speaking."

"Hey, it's Eli." He cleared his throat, shocked at how nervous he suddenly was. "I need your help."

Eli stood in front of the welcome desk at the nursing home, his hands shoved deep into his jeans pockets, his present for his mom tucked under his arm, feeling very much like a kid called to the principal's office. He'd prayed the excitement he'd felt from talking to Nolan, the plans he'd made for seeing Devan, would get him through the next hour or so. And then he'd pulled into the parking lot, his gaze landing on the low sloping roof of the nursing home, and every bit of bliss he'd been riding evaporated.

The nurse behind the desk appeared to be many years younger than himself, but the scowl on her face was well practiced. "The doctor had mentioned that you were coming to visit. We'd expected you a few days ago." She held his gaze in such a way that would have made him tap out if he were in the cage.

"Yeah, sorry about that. I thought she needed some more time to get better before I subjected her to me."

"Of course." Which was clearly nurse-speak for *The only one who needed more time was you, asshole.* Or something like that. "We've had to move her to a room in the dementia wing. Come with me and I'll buzz you in."

There was a smell to the nursing home that always made the hair on his arms stand up. It wasn't offensive, but it wasn't a natural smell either. Cleaning solution, food, and something else that he'd never been able to identify, mixed together and washed over him as he docilely followed the nurse.

"Her condition has worsened since the last time you were here. The doctors aren't sure, but she might have had another mini stroke. But today has been a pretty good day." She swiped her badge and the double doors swung open. "There's a code above the pin pad that you'll need to type in to get out. Your mom is down the hall, third room from the window."

It broke his heart every time they told him about the code. His mom had always been a smart woman with keen eyes. Knowing that she couldn't get out with the information shown in plain sight, was almost too much to believe. "Thanks."

Eli kept his eyes fixed on the end of the hall, not wanting to catch a glimpse of the other patients in the ward. He caught random bits of sounds from televisions and radios as he walked. Game shows seemed to be the preference, something that would have normally driven his mom nuts.

Bad choice of words, asshole.

He stopped in front of his mother's room, taking a quick look at the colorful name tag they'd put up. *Rhonda's Room.* It was covered with flower stickers: roses and tulips, his mom's favorite. Eli closed his eyes for a moment, took a breath, and knocked on the door.

"Hello?" His mom's voice was the same as always.

Eli poked his head around the door, his gaze landing on the too-frail form of his mom sitting in her chair in front of the television. "Hey."

His mom broke out into a smile. "Hi there. Come in, come in. Take my chair."

He had to move fast to stop her from getting up. "Nope, that's your spot. I can sit on the bed." Guiding her back into her seat, he sat as close to her as possible. "How are you feeling?"

She looked at him, suddenly frowning. "You're not a doctor."

His throat tightened. "No. I'm Eli."

She whispered his name over and over, before breaking out into another grin. "Yes, you're Eli. My son. I know you."

He leaned over and kissed her gently on the cheek. "You look good. Have you been flirting with the doctors again? Do I need to warn them off?"

She chuckled as she patted his hand. "I'm quite the catch."

Rhonda McGovern was still beautiful. Her brown hair was pulled back into a bun, no doubt done by one of the caretakers. And while there wasn't the same spark of excitement in her eyes, she seemed at ease.

At least for the moment.

"I brought you something." He retrieved the cylinder from the bed where he'd placed it. "A little something for your room."

The poster had been produced at Stephan's insistence, promo that they'd used for his fight with Caulfield that summer. Eli had been oiled up and made to wear a sleeveless hoodie that showed off more muscle than it hid.

His mom took the poster, clucking her tongue. "Well, isn't this a handsome fella."

"It's me, Mom."

She looked at him, her smile back once more. "So it is."

The doctor had told him on the phone that pictures were a good way to help her keep her memories. The stroke had done serious damage, but every little bit they did helped her. "Can I put it up?"

"Yes." She nodded and looked around. "How about by the window? I always like the sun."

Eli found some tape and put the poster up. "I have an idea." He'd brought a marker with him, but wasn't sure how she'd react. "Can I put my name on this? So you'll remember that it's a picture of me?"

His mom's attention had drifted back to the television, and she was now engrossed in *The Price Is Right*. The little parting of the clouds of her mind had vanished, leaving Eli alone. Ignoring the burning in the back of his throat, he took the marker and wrote in clear block letters in a white spot by his face on the poster.

Eli McGovern. My son.

He wanted nothing more than to leave. There was no point in talking to her now; any conversations they'd have would quickly be forgotten. Turning, he took a step toward the door before changing course to sit back down on the bed beside her.

He was all she had in the world. It didn't matter that she didn't remember him, or that he hadn't been there for her as much as he should have. Eli was here now, and he'd be *damned* if he'd leave her alone.

There'd been so much he'd left behind when he'd moved to Montreal. While he'd ensured his mom was cared for, that didn't take away from the fact that she'd needed him as well. He'd been so busy, so focused on himself, that he'd brushed aside his duties as a son.

And a husband.

"Oh, Plinko!" His mom clapped her hands and looked at him. "Hello."

"Hello." The word came out little more than a choke.

He took her hand and watched the show.

— CHAPTER — SIX

Devan had brought a change of clothing with him to work, which immediately set the girls off. He never bothered with anything other than his uniform unless he was going on a date. Seeing as how that hadn't happened in, well, three years, they were curious to know who the lucky guy was.

The last thing he wanted was to tell them that he was going out on a sort-of date with Eli. When Eli had left Devan, he'd become deadbeat husband number one in their eyes. Over the years, they'd offered more than a bit of advice on how to make the divorce happen. But going out with Eli wasn't exactly something he could keep from them either. If he could sneak out, give a friendly wave on his way past, he'd at least be able to delay the inevitable grilling until tomorrow.

The moment he slipped on his coat, Karen walked into the lunchroom. She took one look at him and grinned. "So who is it? New guy? Blind date? Old lover?"

Devan groaned. "I so don't want to tell you."

Karen raised an eyebrow. "Yeah, so you have to tell me now. Because you suck at secrets."

God, sometimes he hated that everyone knew him so well. "Fine, but you have to promise me not to let anyone else know."

She laughed. "Right. How about I promise to wait until you leave?"

"Fair enough. I'm going out with Eli."

"You're *what*?" Her voice went high enough there was no doubt everyone in the building had heard her. "That bastard finally showed his face again, after all this time, and you're going on a *date* with him? Are you insane?"

Yes, it was most likely that he was. "It's not like that. He came to town to help a friend, and I chased him down. Apparently, his manager hadn't been passing on my messages, or something. He said he'd sign the divorce papers, and offered to take me out as an apology. That's it. Nothing more than him trying to suck up and grovel."

That was at least what Devan had been telling himself Eli would do since the moment he'd closed the door to his apartment. He'd been emotionally crushed for years, felt as though he were carrying a heavy weight on his shoulders that he'd never get rid of. Despite his life with Matthew, there was a piece missing, and Devan knew it had to do with Eli.

Was this a colossal mistake? Probably.

He would know by the end of dinner.

Karen shook her head. "You better get those papers signed fast. He doesn't deserve five minutes of your time. Not after what he did to you."

"I know." The problem was, as angry as Devan was, he knew there was a part of him that was still in love with Eli. Always would be. "But I think we both need this dinner. For closure, if nothing else."

Karen pulled him in for a hug. "You have my number. If you need me to do anything, or if you need to talk after, call me."

"Thanks, hon. I'm sure I'll be fine."

Grabbing his bag, he plastered a smile on his face that he didn't quite feel and headed outside. Eli was leaning against a car, hands in his jeans pockets, waiting for him. His bald head looked freshly shaved, unlike his face, which had a day's worth of scruff on it. The black leather jacket was stretched tight across his muscular arms and chest. As always, Devan couldn't believe that this beautiful man had been remotely interested in him. Devan was thin and as far from an athlete as one could get. Aware of the cold wind, he screwed up his courage and headed over.

"Hey." Devan shifted his duffel bag to his other shoulder. "I wasn't sure where we were going, so I hope I'm dressed okay."

Eli let his gaze drift down Devan's body, making him self-conscious. "Handsome as ever." He moved from the car and opened the door. "We're not going too far."

This was his last chance to back out. He had the divorce papers in his bag, and he knew that if he said no, Eli would sign them and Devan would never have to see him again. Instead, he squeezed the strap of his bag and got into the passenger seat.

Eli was thankful Nolan had suggested the Pear Tree as a place to eat. It was fancy enough to have great atmosphere and food, but relaxed enough that he didn't feel out of place. Eli's size alone tended to turn heads. Being six feet, seven inches tall was one thing, but adding his bulk tended to cause people to stare. Or flee in the opposite direction.

The hostess had given them a booth in the back corner of the restaurant, ensuring that they'd have a certain amount of privacy. Devan looked around once they'd been seated, and Eli was smart enough to realize he was avoiding eye contact.

Could he blame him?

Clearing his throat, Eli opened the menu. "I've never eaten here, but Nolan assured me that the food is good."

Devan shifted in his seat. "I haven't been here either. Never heard of it. I'm sure it's fine."

An awkward silence stretched on for far longer than Eli would have liked. "What's steak fritz?"

Devan snorted, his lips quivering. "You mean steak *frites*?"

"Yeah, that."

"Steak in a sauce and fries. That's all."

"Oh." He liked steak, but it was more of a treat than a regular thing.

When he looked up, Devan was actually smiling. "You never did get the French accent thing right."

"You'd think after living in Montreal for a while I would have picked it up." The second the words left his mouth, Eli regretted them. No sense hiding from what he'd done. "The Quebec fighters made fun of my accent all the time."

Devan's smile faltered. "Why did you go there? I mean, to train?"

"It's the best facility in Canada. One of the best in the world, actually." There were two ways Eli could handle this: he could pretend that him being an utter asshole and leaving Devan hadn't happened, or he could face up to what he'd done. Despite everything, Eli still cared about Devan and knew he owed him the truth. "Would you like to hear about it, or talk about something else?"

It was clear Devan didn't know how to go forward any better than he did. Setting his menu down, he finally met Eli's gaze. "Yeah, I think I would."

The muscles in his neck and back relaxed. "I'll be sure to leave out the gory bits."

"I work with blood on a daily basis. I laugh in the face of gory bits. Hahahahaha." The fake laugh brought a small smile to Eli's face.

The tension bled from the air around them as Eli shared some of the pieces of his life in Montreal. He paused only long enough for them to order drinks and their meals: steak frites for him and sweet potato lasagna for Devan.

Devan asked the occasional question here and there, but mostly let Eli talk. That was the one thing about him Eli had always been amazed by. Devan was one of the few people he'd ever met who could get him talking. There'd never been any pressure to be anyone other than who he was, unlike with the guys at the gym, or with his fans. He wasn't Eli McGovern, in-the-closet MMA fighter, potential champion. He didn't need to know how to say *steak frites* properly, or worry about making sure his socks matched.

He could simply be Eli, fatherless guy whose mom had never quite accepted he was gay.

It was weird how he hadn't realized how hard it had been on him to keep up the tough-guy persona.

"So they took me to a strip club on Saint Catherine Street for my birthday, a female strip club. The guys were pooling their money and got me this crazy lap dance in a private room." Eli shook his head as Devan laughed loudly. "I'm in this scummy little room with this sweet girl, and I had to tell her that I was gay. Instead of getting her vagina in my face, we talked about the university program she was taking at McGill."

Devan had tears in his eyes he was laughing so hard. "Oh my God, I can totally picture that. Was she upset?"

"Not even a little. Apparently, they don't get a lot of breaks, so she appreciated the rest."

"I can't believe that happened to you."

"The problem of not being officially out." That had been the one thing he'd always hated about being a fighter. Stephan had insisted, made continuous comments about it, that if Eli were gay—*and I'm not saying that you are, but if it's the case*—to not mention it.

By the time their food arrived, Eli realized he'd been doing the majority of the talking. "So what about you?"

"What about me?"

From the flash of guilt on Devan's face, Eli realized he'd been keeping him talking so he wouldn't have to share anything. Eli deserved that treatment, but it wouldn't sate his curiosity. "Why don't you tell me a bit about Matthew?"

It was the one thing he'd wanted to know, but he'd been more than a little scared that Devan would get up and walk away rather than give him the answers he hoped for.

Devan stopped eating and began to push the food around his plate. It was one of his nervous ticks, something Eli hadn't seen since the early days of their relationship. "I don't know what you want to know."

This was the part of their relationship that he'd always sucked at. Eli wasn't good with people, never had been. He'd come to rely on Devan to help with small talk, the right questions to ask to make someone feel important, special. So Eli asked the one question that had been turning over in his mind since he'd first laid eyes on Matthew. "Tell me about the day he was born."

For a moment, he wasn't sure Devan was going to give him that, to grant him the privilege of peeking into the life that he could have had. He had no right to push, no matter how desperately he wanted to. But as Eli took his next bite of food, Devan put down his fork and picked up his wineglass.

"It was raining."

Eli swallowed, put his own fork down and did his best to hear everything Devan said, spoken or otherwise.

"Meg was past due, and we'd planned to have her induced the next day. It was a pretty warm day for December, and she'd been having a hard time doing anything. Matthew thought it would be fun to give up the wait at the worst possible time." Devan chuckled and sipped his wine. "Meg and Josh were at the movies. I don't know what they'd gone to see, something bad, knowing their preferences. She'd been craving movie theatre popcorn, and Josh had learned pretty early on not to argue with her when a craving hit. Her water broke right in the middle of the film."

Knowing Meg, she'd probably laughed at the irony of the situation. She was pretty awesome like that. "I hope she got to finish her popcorn?"

"Took it with her into the maternity room." Devan laughed. "So I got a call from them at ten thirty at night telling me to get my ass to the hospital. I was so freaked out that I nearly forgot the baby bag. By the time I caught a cab and made it to the hospital, she was well into labor. I had to sit and wait with Josh."

Eli hadn't known Meg's husband very long before he'd left. They'd only been married a short time, and Josh wasn't exactly the type of guy Eli would hang out with. "He must have thought the whole thing was weird."

"Not really. Well, Josh really isn't into kids. I think he saw this as a win-win for him. Meg got to be a part of a child's life, but they didn't have any of the responsibility. Well, unless I die. They will get Matthew if anything happens to me."

The air seemed to escape Eli's lungs. "What if he's mine? Don't I get a say in this?"

Devan blinked. "No. You don't. You didn't want anything to do with me or a baby. You left. Why would I think you'd want anything to do with him, let alone think you would be an ideal father for my son?" Devan sat back and fingered the edge of the plate. "Honestly, I think this was a mistake. You should sign the divorce papers so I can go."

Eli's heart pounded so hard he thought for a moment it would crack through his chest. "I'm sorry."

"For what?"

This was it, his one and only opportunity to say the right words. "I should never have walked out on you the way that I did."

"No shit." Devan cleared his throat.

"I . . . I never told you that Mom had another minor stroke. A few days before the miscarriage."

Devan's eyes grew wide. "*What*? Why didn't you say something?"

"Because you'd been so focused on Meg and the baby, and I knew work was stressing you out. Mom wasn't going to get any better, and you didn't need yet another thing on your plate."

"Jesus, Eli."

"I spoke to Stephan, and he suggested I come train in Montreal full-time. I didn't know what to do. Then when Meg . . . I should have talked to you about how I'd been feeling long before that night. I don't do emotions very well. I let them control me rather than face them. The excuses don't matter. You didn't deserve that. I'm sorry."

He didn't know if he deserved Devan's forgiveness, but he was going to damn well make the effort. Eli got up and came around to Devan's side of the booth. Rather than say anything, he reached into the duffel bag and fished out the divorce papers. "Do you have a pen?"

"I haven't left yet." Devan's voice shook. "You haven't even read them."

"I know. But this is one more thing that should have been handled long ago. I don't know why Stephan never told me you were trying to get in touch, and I hate that he did that. He had no fucking right to take your choice to be free of me away from you." He reached into the bag and pulled out a pen, quickly finding all the spots that required his signature. He slid the papers into the envelope before returning them. "There. It's now your decision. If you want to finalize the divorce, you can send those to your lawyer, and it's done."

He should have immediately gotten back up and returned to his side of the table. But this was only the second time in years that he'd been this close to Devan, legs and arms touching, hands close enough to caress. Eli was selfish enough to want to take advantage of this small moment. It wasn't until he saw the waiter heading over that he knew he needed to move.

"What time did you say you needed to be back home?"

Devan looked at his phone as the table was cleared. "Oh shit. It's after seven."

Eli didn't know the rules for having a babysitter, but being late was a pretty obvious no-no. "Can I get the bill please? We have to jet."

"I better call and let Sandy know I'm on my way. Shit, this is . . . Hi, Sandy." Devan was up and moving toward the washrooms.

Eli didn't bother waiting, got up, and went to the front to pay for the meal. He'd barely finished when Devan came racing over, eyes wide and panicked. "I have to get a cab. Sandy said Matthew was fussing terribly in the last half hour."

"I'll drive you." Eli pulled his jacket on.

"It's probably him teething. She got worried but didn't want to interrupt my date." He took out his phone and hit a taxi app.

"I said I'd drive you." When Devan started to protest, Eli reached out and covered his phone. "I'm here and free. I know where you live, so it's not a secret. Please, let me do this."

Devan's mental battle was plain as day on his face. "Yeah. Okay. Thanks."

With a nod to the hostess, he pressed his hand to Devan's back as they walked outside. The car was parked in a lot down the street, but they didn't do much in the way of talking. Devan continued to look down at his phone, and Eli was far too unsure of what to say in the current situation.

The ride to Devan's apartment was quiet as he texted with his sitter. As Eli pulled into the visitor parking spot, Devan turned to say something before his mouth snapped shut. Yeah, Eli wasn't going to let that go. Leaning in, he placed a soft kiss to Devan's cheek.

"I'll be training down at Ringside for the next several weeks. Seems I have a last-minute match that's come up in the beginning of December. I don't want to keep you, but if you need me for anything, call me. Or text."

Devan's eyes were wide, and a blush covered his cheeks. "Thank you."

"I hope your son is doing okay."

"Thank you for dinner." Devan hesitated before opening the door and getting out.

Eli watched Devan race across the parking lot to the apartment building. Despite him signing the papers, despite every which way he'd screwed up with Devan, tonight hadn't seemed like an ending.

No, for the first time in forever, it felt as though he'd done something exactly right.

CHAPTER SEVEN

Devan paid Sandy extra for keeping Matthew later than intended, and quickly scooped his son into his arms. Matthew's gums were swollen and he was drooling up a storm, confirming what he'd suspected about this being a teething episode.

He got onto the couch, Matthew resting on his chest with his ear over Devan's heart, and tried to relax. Today had been such a whirlwind of emotions, he knew he was going to need time to process everything. Like the fact that he was divorced.

Well, he would be as soon as he sent in those papers.

Matthew began sucking his thumb as Devan's gaze drifted over to his duffel bag and the papers inside. When Eli had slid over and retrieved them, Devan hadn't known what to think. Sure, Stephan had kept Eli in the dark, but he'd still been away long enough to realize something like this had happened. He should have reached out to Devan long before now.

But from the moment they'd sat down for supper, Devan had seen a difference in Eli. Before he'd left, Eli had always been closed off and reserved. Eli tonight had been contrite, talkative. Eli had said more about his mom and his dreams in the hour and a half they'd been eating than he had in an entire month prior to their split. Devan didn't know if it was Eli's leaving that had changed him, or his coming home.

"What the hell am I going to do?" He stroked Matthew's soft hair, needing the baby scent to soothe his soul.

There was still the fact that Matthew could very well be Eli's. Devan hadn't let his brain go to that possibility too much over the past year and a half. Until now, it hadn't really mattered if he was the biological father or not. Eli wasn't in the picture and had made it abundantly clear that he wanted nothing to do with kids.

But the Eli he'd seen tonight was a different man than the one he'd been married to.

Curiosity about what Eli had gone through recently finally got to him. He'd made it a point of blocking out all things MMA the moment Eli had left him, so he wasn't sure when his last fight had been.

Careful not to wake Matthew, he pulled out his phone and hit the microphone. "Okay Google, when did Eli McGovern last fight?"

"Eli McGovern's last MMA fight was on August 25, 2016. His opponent was Jay 'The Dragon' Caulfield, who he defeated at two minutes and twenty-three seconds of the second round."

There was a bunch of other information, pre- and post-interview bravado, interviews with managers, blah, blah, blah. From what was listed here, Caulfield sounded like a complete asshole. He'd find his opponent's weakness and would exploit it in both the media and in the ring. No wonder Eli had to be careful when it came to his sexuality. If a guy like Caulfield got wind of it, he'd turn Eli's career into a sideshow.

And this was the same asshole who Eli was going to fight in December? Why the hell would he agree to something like that? *Probably Stephan's brilliant idea or something.* For such a tough-ass man, Eli could be a complete pushover when it came to some things.

With a few quick swipes, he brought up Eli's number and stared at it. Eli had given a large portion of his life to his fighting career, and when they'd been together, Devan hadn't taken much interest in it beyond knowing when Eli was training. Devan had been so focused on Eli's faults that he'd never taken much stock in his own shortcomings. What harm could it do to talk to Eli about the fight? Especially after how well supper had gone. He was only reaching out as an interested friend.

Yeah, that was all this was.

Swiping, he brought up the text app. *Hey. I was a bit upset and didn't thank you for bringing me home.*

He waited, hoping that Eli was still awake. Time ticked on, and Devan started to nod off. When his phone buzzed, he jerked awake, which caused Matthew to squirm.

Just saw this. I was working on fixing the master bedroom at mom's. You did thank me. But you're still welcome. There was a pause before another message popped up. *How's he doing?*

Excitement made his nerves tingle as he thumbed out a response. *He's fine. Teething as I'd suspected. I should probably put him in the crib soon.*

Where r you now?

Couch. He likes it out here when he's upset.

I'm glad it wasn't anything serious.

Devan kissed the top of Matthew's head. *I've been reading up on you.*

Oh?

Got curious. Devan felt his face flush. "God, you're such a kid."

There was a slightly longer pause before Eli responded. *I could have told you. Only have to ask.*

Much like he'd been at supper, Devan found himself at an unexpected loss for words. Sure, they hadn't spoken to one another in three years, but this was still *Eli*. Devan tapped his thumb on the edge of his phone before finally typing. *Is that Caulfield guy as bad as the internet says?*

Eventually Eli responded. *Yeah, he's an ass. But Stephan has worked things out for this rematch. Big opportunity.*

Matthew squirmed against him, and for a moment Devan thought they were about to go through another round of crying. Eventually, he would have to move Matthew to his crib, and it was better to do that when he was mostly asleep.

I have to put M in bed. Promise to look after yourself.

Tossing his phone onto the coffee table, Devan carefully got up and moved Matthew to bed. Twenty minutes and some expected fussing later, Devan was exhausted. He needed to plug his phone in, then head to bed himself. Nothing said *I'm rocking the single parent thing* like going to bed at nine o'clock.

The message light was flashing when he picked it up. Eli had sent a final message, one that Devan didn't know quite what to make of.

I'm training at Ringside. 5 days a wk. In case u need anything.

An invitation? Devan walked to his bedroom, trying to figure out what to do with this particular piece of information. He set his phone on his nightstand, plugged it in but didn't respond. Meg would kick his ass for even considering doing anything with Eli. Dinner tonight had served a purpose, and now he was free. Finally, he could go out on dates and not feel guilty about being technically married. Not that he actually went on dates, but he totally could. And if they wanted to come back to his place and get intimate, he could do that without wondering if he was technically cheating on a man who'd walked away from him without a backward glance.

Not that he did that either.

After getting naked, he turned off his lamp, slid beneath his cool sheets, and closed his eyes. The temperature change did him a world of good, helping slow his mind down. As screwed up as it was, he still had feelings for Eli. He probably always would. The real question was, did he want to put his heart back out there, available for Eli to hurt him once again?

God, what's the matter with me? Date Eli again after what he did?

He needed to leave Eli in the past and get on with his life.

Closing his eyes, Devan reached down and wrapped his hand around his soft cock. Nothing like a good jerk to clear his head and help him sleep. A few tugs was all it took to get the blood flowing, his shaft slowly filling out in his grasp. Devan had a go-to fantasy that always did the trick in a timely fashion. He relaxed into the mental picture as he began to stroke.

He was in a bar with his back to the crowd. People were moving behind him, the occasional brush of an arm or body against him. It was hot, and he needed to get cool. In his fantasy, Devan pulled his shirt off, his nipples hardening from the change in air temperature. In reality, he pushed the sheet down so he could brush his nipple with his free hand.

He pictured a man coming up behind him. He couldn't see his face—he never did—but he could feel the length of his body, the heat rolling off him to wash over Devan's back.

"So handsome." The voice was close to his ear, sending shivers through him. "I want to touch you."

Devan never spoke, he didn't need to. Now naked in his dream, he opened his legs wide and knew the man would help him. He increased the rate of his strokes, driving his arousal to the point where he knew he'd come.

But the fantasy, the same scenario that he'd run through his mind for years now, changed tonight. Devan pictured a long, muscular arm reaching down to cup his balls. A firm chest pressed hard to his back, the scrape of a stubble-covered chin against his cleanly shaven cheek.

"I want to hear you moan."

It was Eli's voice. Eli's hand between his legs.

It should have been a turnoff. It wasn't.

Devan moaned, the fantasy morphing into memories. Eli wrapping his arms around him as they fucked against the counter in the kitchen. The low, rumbling sounds he'd make when he was turned on, close to orgasm. Devan's heart pounded hard, and sweat beaded on his skin as his orgasm crept closer.

He missed the feeling of Eli's body wrapped around him. The scent of him as they'd make love, something he'd long pushed from his memory, was back. Devan tried to slow things down, not wanting to come to long-forgotten memories. He didn't need them, not when he had the man who'd stolen his heart back in his life.

Eli looked older now, more muscular than before. Devan pictured the muscles and how they'd flex if Eli were to grab him, stroke his cock. That devilish smile Eli always got when he was up to no good was still there. His gentleness that seemingly contrasted the pure power that lay behind his every touch.

His hand flew over his shaft, and Devan knew he wasn't going to last. Thoughts left him as the overwhelming surge of pleasure slammed through him. The first spurts of come shot from him to land in warm beads across his hand and groin as his orgasm rolled over him. He squeezed his lips shut, trying to keep the noises he so desperately wanted to make trapped inside.

As quickly as his release came, Devan collapsed. The sheets were no longer cool and comforting. His body was sweaty, come now stuck to his pubic hair in a way that would be not so fun to clean up. And none of that mattered. He'd had one of the best orgasms he'd had in a long time. Inner peace gave his body a chance to relax. His heart and head were on a temporary vacation, giving him the opportunity to drift.

It took him longer than normal to shake himself out of his haze, to reach over and grab the packet of baby wipes he kept there for emergency Matthew accidents. Thankfully, they were multipurpose.

As he cleaned himself up, Devan couldn't help but wonder what all this had meant. It wasn't surprising that he was still sexually attracted to Eli. Shit, he'd have to be blind not to find his physical appearance sexy. But there was no way he could do anything about it. Eli could live in his fantasy material for the rest of Devan's life, and that would be good enough.

Except . . .

Except Devan was lonely.

Rolling over, he turned off the light and lay there in the dark. Sleep refused to come, mostly because his mind was mulling over the problem of his technically ex-husband. Devan was past the point of wanting Eli to make amends. Wasn't he? There was no way their relationship could work out any differently if they tried again. Right?

Devan adjusted his pillow, giving it a good punch, before settling back down.

"Okay, brain. You need to shut up now."

Except his brain had one last thought. A final thing to keep Devan awake.

Eli had looked as lonely as Devan felt.

CHAPTER EIGHT

It had been a week since Eli had last heard from Devan, but he wasn't really surprised that Devan hadn't reached out. Eli had given him what he'd needed—the paperwork was signed and no doubt with a lawyer or en route to some courthouse or whatever to be processed. Why would he bother to say anything to Eli at all? Eli hadn't done anything to earn Devan's trust since returning.

And, really, what the hell was he hoping for? A chance to get back together? Devan had spent years carving out a life that didn't involve him. Looking at it from the outside, Eli craved a measure of closeness with someone the way Devan had with Matthew, but that didn't mean he deserved it.

Eli worked out his disappointment at Ringside. While he loved Zack and the gym, it wasn't exactly the right setup for what he needed to be ready for his match with Caulfield in three weeks. Ideally, he would have gone back to Montreal and lived at the gym there until the time came for the fight. But despite the numerous emails and calls from Stephan begging him to do exactly that, Eli wasn't about to leave his mom. She'd actually recognized him yesterday when he'd gone into her room for his visit. That bright smile and sparkle in her eyes was all he needed to solidify his resolve.

Ringside Gym would have to do.

The heavy bag swung gently from the previous kick he'd landed. It felt good to stretch his muscles, to feel the impact of skin on canvas. He hadn't been at it long, having waited until close to closing time before starting. Zack and Nolan were off somewhere, and he hadn't seen Grady since his arrival. There were only a few others working out, though Eli was aware of them watching him. A young guy in the back had been mirroring his moves, something that never bothered Eli. A kid had to learn somehow, and not everyone could afford a trainer.

Focus, asshole.

Bringing his hands up to a guard position, he landed two jabs and a cross before connecting with a roundhouse. *Bang, bang, thwap* sounded behind him. Reaching out to grab the bag, he peered over at the kid on the other side of the gym, who, as expected, was doing the same. Eli turned so he was now on the other side of the bag and able to see the kid. The young man averted his gaze, so Eli waited until he finally looked up once more.

Getting into his stance, he waited for the kid to mimic him, giving him a nod and a small smile when the kid got into the correct position. He then held up his arms to guard his face, encouraging the kid to lift them higher, before repeating the move. Jab, jab, cross, roundhouse. The kid was shaky, but pulled it off pretty well.

"Do that five more times, then switch feet and lead with your left hand." Eli nodded at the kid again, getting a kick out of the way the young guy grinned.

"Why don't I have you coaching here?" Zack stood in the office doorway, clearly having observed the entire exchange.

"Because I won't be around for long and you don't want to upset your clients."

"Naw, that's not it." Zack snapped his fingers. "I know, it's because you're an asshole."

"Hey now, that's one of my best features." Eli gave the heavy bag another few hits before heading over to Zack. "What did I do now?"

Zack nodded toward the office, so Eli trailed along behind him. His hands were sore despite being wrapped up, which spoke volumes as to how out of shape he was. Given how little time he had to get ready for the fight in a few weeks, that wasn't a good thing.

"I got a Google alert on the gym this morning. Your appearance here was mentioned, as was your upcoming fight." Zack frowned. "When did all that happen?"

"Not long ago. I'm taking you up on your offer to train here."

"Cool. Whatever you need." The look on Zack's face told him that there was more to this conversation than curiosity about his match.

"Spit it out, dude."

"Did you meet up with Devan?"

The question hit harder than a sucker punch. "I did."

"And?"

"And I took him out to supper, apologized, and signed the divorce papers."

Zack nodded, but rather than a look of approval, Eli was surprised to see disappointment. "I'm glad you did the right thing."

Eli began to pull the wrap from around his hand. "Sure. Stephan put me in a bad spot, but it was still on me. What else could I do?"

"I don't know, maybe you could make an attempt to win him back?"

"Why the hell would I bother? He's got a kid, his own place; he doesn't need me back in his life to fuck it up."

Zack's head shot up. "He's got a kid? How?"

"Well, when a man loves a woman, they hug each other really tight and make a baby."

"See, asshole."

"I am." Eli quickly filled him in on everything Devan had said. "His name's Matthew."

Zack sat on the edge of his desk, his face a tangle of emotions. "So you're telling me that there's a chance this kid is yours, and you're not going to do anything about it?"

"What the hell can I do?" He'd spent days going through scenarios in his mind, begging Devan to take him back, leaving Toronto for good and never returning. "If the kid is mine, I have no right to force myself back into his life. I left him. Told him I didn't want a family. I can't change my mind now."

"Dude, you were hurting. I wasn't surprised that you had a breakdown. Other couples who've had to deal with miscarriages have had to work through similar issues and no, not all couples make it. But you went a little scorched-earth on your life here. That caught me off guard."

It had caught Eli off guard as well. Months after he'd left Devan and moved to Montreal, he'd had one of those *oh fuck* moments. Half-naked in a locker room, the severity of what he'd done to Devan, to their relationship, had hit him hard. He'd been terrified the night of Meg's miscarriage. Partially because of what had happened to her, but also because he'd known Devan would want to try again. He'd told Devan that he didn't want to have a child, but the truth was, he'd been scared of *losing* a child again, and maybe even more scared that the next time would work and he'd end up being a father. With his history, he'd be a train wreck of a father. The idea of having that level of responsibility for another person's well-being . . . Eli didn't think he could do it.

From that moment on, anger had become his default mode and had helped fuel his fights for the years to follow. All because he'd walked away from the best thing that had ever happened to him, because he'd been too much of a coward to tell Devan what he was really feeling.

Eli dropped the wrap to the floor and went to work freeing his other hand. "He deserves better than me."

"I think that's up for him to decide."

"I told him where I was going to be for the next few weeks. He never responded after that. I have no intention of pushing him. If he never wants to see me again, then that's fine with me." It wasn't, but he'd tied his own hands three years ago when he'd left.

"Well, lucky for you, he seems to have had a change of heart." Zack nodded beyond Eli, causing him to turn around to see.

There was Devan, dressed in his uniform and looking around like a lost child.

"Shit." Eli stood, but his feet refused to take him toward the man he still loved more than anything in the world.

Devan wasn't in horrible shape, but he wasn't one to do much beyond the occasional run. He certainly had never understood what drove Eli to push his body to its limit. Standing there, looking tired from what must have been a long day, Devan was more fish out of water than anyone else who'd come to Ringside over the years.

"Are you going to go see him?" Zack took his seat behind his desk and pointedly looked at his computer screen. "I'm sure he won't stay long if he doesn't see you."

With a huff, Eli forced himself to move. The moment he stepped out of the office, Devan's gaze snapped to him. He'd always been able to do that: find him when he wanted. It didn't matter if they'd been separated in a massive crowd, it wouldn't take Devan long to locate him. It was one of the first things about him that Eli had fallen in love with. He waited until he was standing right in front of Devan before he gave him a small smile. "Hey. I'm surprised to see you."

A blush covered Devan's cheeks. "Honestly, I'm surprised I'm here."

"Is there something wrong? Is Matthew okay?"

Devan smiled. "The little terror is fine. And is now sporting a brand-new front tooth. Looks adorable." Devan whipped out his phone and showed the picture of Matthew and a stuffed animal on his home screen. "Look at that face."

Eli's heart melted at the sight of him. "He's sweet."

"I also realized when I was here the other day that I really need to spend some more time looking after myself. It's so easy to make everything about him. I thought it might be fun to sign up for the gym. Work off some of my work stress." Devan looked around, his eyes landing on the ring. "Not sure this is the right place for me though."

"Lots of opportunity for beginners. Zack is hiring some personal trainers. He can make some recommendations." Eli braced his hands on his hips. "I can train you if you'd like."

Devan's eyes widened. "Ah, really?"

Eli shrugged. "Only if you want. I'm pretty good at what I do, and I won't charge you, either. So you get the best of both worlds."

"I'm not sure."

The kid who'd been mimicking his moves earlier was now watching their exchange intently. "Let's go someplace private and we can talk."

The yoga studio that Nolan was working so hard to get open was currently empty. Another few weeks and everything would be in place for classes to start, and Eli had no doubt they'd be full. For now, the room made the perfect place for them to have a private conversation.

Eli was hyperaware of every move Devan made. Devan clutched the strap of his duffel bag, as though it were some sort of lifeline. Maybe it was. Devan had always kept his discomfort hidden from the world, from Eli. It was as though he never wanted to burden others with his problems; he'd been hardwired to take care of everyone else and put himself second.

The door to the yoga room was open, but there were currently no workers inside. Ushering Devan in, Eli shut the door. "We can talk here."

Devan walked into the room, his gaze passing over everything. "Not quite what I'd expected at a boxing gym."

"It's a great way to build core strength with no impact. It was Nolan's idea." When Devan frowned at him, Eli clarified, "Zack's partner."

Devan gaped. "Wait, Zack *I'm the boss don't fuck with me* Anderson has a boyfriend?"

"They're living together."

Devan laughed. "No way. I absolutely need to meet this guy. I never thought anyone would be able to tolerate Zack's moods. Wait, was he the guy at the door on the day you were signing autographs?"

"That's him. I think he's off today, or else I'd introduce you. Well, I haven't seen him since I got here a few hours ago." Eli pressed his back to the closest mirror and enjoyed the privilege of being able to simply watch Devan. "I'm still a bit surprised that you're here."

Adjusting his duffel bag on his shoulder, Devan's gaze flicked from Eli's to a spot over his shoulder and back. "I . . . I tried a few times to text you, but everything I wrote sounded juvenile. I wanted to see how you were making out with the training."

Eli frowned. "I'm good."

With a shake of his head, Devan set his duffel bag on the floor and walked over to him. "You look tired. I know I don't know much about MMA fights, but three weeks isn't a lot of time to train." Devan crossed his arms, and cocked his head to the side. "I hate to see you pushing yourself too hard."

It wasn't what he'd expected to hear, the concern and caring. Suddenly, the urge to leave the room pressed against him. "I'm fine. Caulfield won't know what hit him."

Devan was only half a foot away, maybe less. His small frame was no match for Eli; he could be easily moved aside if Eli wanted to escape. But there was something about the worry in Devan's eyes that kept him nailed to his spot. No one else had ever looked at him that way. Not the doctors and trainers who were supposed to care for him.

"Do you have anyone caring for you?" Devan lifted his hand, as though he were going to touch Eli. But as suddenly as he moved, he let it fall back to his side.

It was that single halted gesture that caused the tension building inside Eli to snap. Before he questioned what he was doing, he reached out, took Devan by the shoulders, and spun him so he was now pressed against the mirror. With his breath coming out in short pants, Eli glanced down into Devan's surprised gaze. He slowly moved his hands from Devan's shoulders to the mirror, bracketing his head.

"Why do you care?" Eli wanted desperately to kiss him. Wanted to know if his mouth still tasted of coffee and cream. Wanted to hear that little moan Devan always made when he was trying to hold back his arousal and failing.

"I don't know." Devan's tongue darted across his bottom lip. "I should leave."

Eli let his arm closest to the door drop from the mirror. "I'm not stopping you. Go."

Devan didn't move.

Nothing else mattered in that moment: not their past, not the idea that Matthew might be his son, not the ache in his heart. All that mattered was him, Devan, and the fact that he was going to kiss Devan.

Leaning forward slowly so Devan would know what he was doing, he lowered his mouth. At the last second Devan turned his face away, and Eli's lips landed on the side of his neck. That was fine.

The little bite was gentle enough not to leave much of a mark. Devan gasped, but didn't pull away. Eli then ran his tongue up the side of his neck, the familiar taste of Devan's skin after a hard day at work stirring long-forgotten memories. When he slid the tip of his tongue over Devan's pulse point, he could feel the thudding of blood racing.

"Let me kiss you." Eli spoke the words on Devan's skin. He wanted to pull Devan against him, feel Devan's body on his. The few inches that separated them might as well be a mile for all the satisfaction it gave him.

"Eli ... I ..."

"I'll let you go if that's what you want. But, right now, the only thing I can think of is kissing you. I can't get it out of my mind."

He'd woken up most nights, the fleeting remnants of dreams fading from memory, all of them revolving around Devan. It was a unique kind of torture, knowing that the source of his misery was of his own making. Slowly, he moved closer until their chests, their thighs, were pressed together.

Devan sighed before turning his face to Eli's. "This doesn't change anything. I still haven't forgiven you."

"Yup." Eli brushed his mouth against Devan's, trying and failing to keep his eyes opened. "I'll work on that."

The kiss was soft and hard all at once. Devan's lips were smooth, a contrast to Eli's. He reached up and cupped Devan's cheek, enjoying the light prickle of stubble that had formed. Devan tensed beneath him, so Eli deepened the kiss until he relaxed once more.

Passion, something Eli hadn't felt with any other man, sparked to life inside him. Like the furnace being turned on in a long-cold house, something warmed up deep inside his chest.

Devan moaned softly as he slid his hand up Eli's arm. The skin-on-skin contact sent a wave a lust rolling through him, and without thinking, Eli pressed his thickening cock against Devan.

That was the moment when reality decided to rear its ugly head. It came in the form of Grady Barnes.

"Oh shit. I didn't know anyone was in here."

Devan jerked away from Eli, his face flushed and his eyes wide. He pushed at Eli, giving him no choice but to step away. Eli sighed. "Grady." *Little shit.*

It took a moment for Devan to straighten up and adjust his uniform. "Ah. Hi."

Eli didn't know Grady well. Aside from that time at the bar, he'd only spoken with him a few times at the gym, mostly because he was dating Max. He was a nice enough guy, but more of a player than Eli usually bothered with. Devan looked at Grady for a moment before slapping his hand over his mouth. "Oh my God, you're Grady Barnes."

Whenever anyone recognized Grady, he preened. "I am, handsome." He sauntered over and held out his hand. "Max tells me I'm not allowed to flirt with his friends anymore, but I can't help it sometimes." He winked at Eli. "And who might you be?"

"Devan. Devan Walsh." He shook Grady's hand, but suddenly went awkward. "I'm Eli's ex-husband."

Grady cocked an eyebrow as he looked between them. "Right. Well, I clearly interrupted something, so I'll leave you to it."

Devan stepped away, making a beeline for his duffel bag. "I need to get going. My babysitter is expecting me."

"I'll come with you."

Eli started to move, but Devan shook his head. "No. But if you can let Zack know that I want a membership, I'd appreciate it."

He wasn't going to disappear on him; Devan would be *here*. "Sure."

The look Grady shot Eli was nothing short of a silent *Dude, you have some explaining to do*. "I'll walk you out. I came up here to grab a paper the contractor left by mistake." Getting what he came for, he led Devan to the door.

Eli watched, wanting nothing more than to race after him, but knowing it would do him no good. "Can I text you later?"

Devan hesitated at the door before nodding. "After seven. That's when Matthew goes down."

It wasn't much, but it gave Eli hope. "I'll talk to you then."

Standing alone in the empty yoga studio, for the first time in a long while, Eli felt a ray of hope.

= CHAPTER =
NINE

Matthew was a very unhappy baby. This in itself wasn't anything abnormal these days, but Devan couldn't focus on anything but him when there was a problem. Eli had sent him a text twenty minutes ago, one that he'd read but in no way had time to answer. Currently, Matthew was chewing a no-longer-cold teething ring while clutching Mr. Fuzzy's floppy ear in his other hand.

Devan fell back onto the couch and stared down at his son. If someone had told him how soul draining it was to be a single parent, he might have reconsidered. Thankfully, his ignorance had been firmly in place. No matter how tired he got, or frustrated he was, Matthew was the one thing in the world he wanted more than anything.

Except, perhaps, a nap. He'd kill for a nap.

And maybe some ice cream.

His phone buzzed again from where it had slipped between the cushions on the couch. It took a minute to rescue it from its prison, though it came out covered in Cheerio crumbs. Eli's name was on his home screen indicator. It was weird how dueling feelings of dread and excitement swirled inside him. His logical side and his romantic side at complete odds over what to do.

Eli was an asshole.

There was no doubt in Devan's mind that his husband— ex-husband—person who'd broken his heart had changed from the cold, distant man he'd been before he left. Back when they'd first started dating, Eli was the typical tough guy, the person no one would dare mess with. Not that they went out on the town very often. Eli stayed in the closet, and Devan couldn't imagine he'd come out anytime soon. Not with his career so close to exploding. He was hard and unwavering when he got something in his head.

Eli was also one of the sweetest people Devan had ever met.

That was the man he'd fallen in love with. The man he'd run into at a blood drive and hadn't been able to take his eyes off. The man who'd been downright shy when asking if Devan had anyone special in his life. *Girlfriend? Boyfriend?* Their whirlwind, but mostly private, courtship that had quickly turned passionate.

That was the Eli he wanted back.

Matthew let out a sound that could have passed for either a moan or a sigh before dropping his head forward onto his blanket. With his butt in the air, he closed his eyes, and the apartment went quiet.

Devan smiled, and the tension bled from his muscles. He turned on his phone and once again read the messages from Eli.

I wanted to say that I'm sorry for kissing you earlier.

I wanted to say it, but it would be lying.

How the hell was he supposed to respond to that? It wasn't until he read the third message that Devan's heart pounded.

I dream about you.

His thumbs hovered over the keyboard, but his mind was a total blank on what to say. No matter what happened going forward, Devan wouldn't forget about the past, about what Eli had done to him. He wanted this, but he didn't want to ever be in that position of heartbreak ever again. *Fool me once, shame on you . . .*

With a glance at Matthew's sleeping face, Devan thumbed *hi.*

Eli's response came quickly. *Everything ok?*

Teething is a bitch. I got your texts.

And?

Devan sighed. *And I can't forget about what happened 3 yrs ago. Too much @ stake.*

The pause was a lot longer this time, and for a moment, Devan wasn't sure Eli would respond. Eventually a simple *oh* came back.

Shit, that hadn't come across right. *I mean if we r going to do whatever this is, things will have to b different. I need 2 b able to trust u.*

Eli's response came much faster. *Yeah. I know.*

There will have to be rules.

I can follow rules.

R u sure? The Eli he remembered had always loved pushing the boundaries of everything in his life.

I am. What's the 1ˢᵗ one?

Devan hadn't actually thought that far ahead. But now that he did, there were things that he knew needed to be said. *This is only you and me. Matthew is off-limits. Don't want him to get used to you if you leave.* He didn't bother to say *again.*

Agreed.

Now that Devan's brain had kick-started, the list of things he wanted to protect himself from was far too long. Better to play things simple and smart.

Rule 2. I can call things off at any time. If I don't like where things are headed, I'm out.

Agreed.

Rule 3. Whatever this is, given what's happened in the past, I can't be exclusive. I'm free to date other men and so are you.

A pause. *Agreed.*

Devan huffed as he wiggled deeper into the cushions. That had been way easier than he'd thought. Not because he wanted to establish a bunch of hoops for Eli to jump through, but because he figured there'd be some pushback. Maybe Eli really wanted to try being a couple again.

Maybe.

Or maybe things would end up being exactly as they were before.

That was why he didn't want to have Eli around Matthew. Not because Matthew would necessarily form a bond with Eli and would be heartbroken if he was no longer there—though knowing his son, he probably would—but because Devan didn't think he'd be able to bear seeing the two of them together. The thought that Eli might fit neatly back into his little family, that Eli would slip easily into the role that he'd so casually discarded, and then potentially walk away again? No, that wasn't something Devan would allow.

But a date? Something on his own terms? Well, he'd be willing to give that a shot.

Eli hadn't said anything for a few minutes, and Devan was curious what he was doing. With a quick glance at Matthew, he pressed the phone button and dialed Eli.

"I thought you couldn't talk?" No hello or any other pleasantry. Typical.

"The Tylenol has kicked in, and he's fallen asleep. As long as I talk quietly, it should be good." There was an odd scraping sound coming from the receiver. "What's that noise?"

"I'm crack filling the kitchen. I wanted to get it done tonight so I could sand it down tomorrow after training."

"You don't know how to stop, do you?"

"It's too quiet in this house, and I can't sit still."

Eli had always been a doer. While Devan loved cooking and puttering around the house, there hadn't been much for him to finish by the time he'd get back from a shift at the clinic. If Eli was home, everything would be cleaned, organized, and meals made. It was one of the many things he missed about him. "How's your mom doing?"

"Good. I saw her yesterday, and we went out for a walk in the park area. I swear some days she knows exactly who I am. But there are lots where she doesn't."

Devan could hear the heartbreak in Eli's voice. "I'm sorry you're going through that. If you ever need company to go with you—"

"Thanks." Eli's voice shook as he spoke, forcing him to clear his throat. More scraping and a *thunk* echoed through the receiver. "How about tomorrow night?"

"For what?"

"Our next date."

He'd made Rule 3 for a very specific reason. But that didn't make this any easier for him to say. "I can't."

"Why?"

"I already have a date."

When the girls at the clinic had heard that Eli was back and trying to win Devan over, they'd gone into an uproar. Surrounded by five peeved women who demanded that he get online and arrange a date with *anyone* but Eli was an experience he never hoped to relive. However, they did make an excellent point. "I haven't dated anyone since you left. I need to give myself options. I need to get back out there and see what I've been missing." *I need to see if I can fall in love with anyone other than you.* "I would hope you can appreciate that."

Eli didn't say anything. He was still there—his heavy breathing gave him away. No doubt he was trying to process everything Devan had said.

"I won't be able to get another babysitter until next week. We can go out to dinner then if you'd like."

A huff echoed through the receiver. "Sure. It will give me time to practice. As much as I'd like to use you as an excuse, I don't have a lot of spare time to train."

Devan couldn't help being pleased at the annoyance in Eli's voice. "Don't push yourself too hard."

"I better go."

"Okay. I'll talk to you soon."

When Eli hung up, Devan smiled. Yes, there was a part of him that wanted to go on this date tomorrow night, wanted to see if he'd feel that same spark that always ignited when he looked at Eli. But there was a larger part that was happy to simply make Eli squirm. Eli had been cruel, the way he'd walked out of his life, so the least Devan could do was show Eli that he couldn't simply return and expect Devan to do cartwheels and invite him back.

No, it would do Eli good to suffer a bit.

His phone buzzed, and Devan flipped it over to see if Eli had texted him again. This time the message was from Meg. *Josh & I having people over on the weekend. U & M want to come?*

Shit, he hadn't said anything to Meg about what had happened with Eli. No doubt this was her way to get him to talk to her.

M's teething. Probably not a good idea.

Poor baby. How R things?

Good. Date tomorrow.

Really?? Awesome!

Date next week with Eli . . .

His phone rang. Meg started talking as soon as he picked up. "You're going out with that asshole? Hon, *why?*"

Devan sighed. "He's signed the papers. Apparently, his manager had been the one blocking communication between us."

"That smells like a lot of bullshit. Fuck him. Are you going out with him tomorrow too?"

"No, that's a dating app thing. Girls at work forced me."

"Good." He could practically hear Meg biting her nails. "You should walk away from Eli."

"I know."

"But you won't."

He sighed again. "I can't really explain it, but he's different. He's still Eli, but . . . I don't know. When he saw Matthew—"

"You let him see Mattie?" The horror in her voice was clear.

"It's a long story, but yes, he knows about Matthew. I swear something changed in him when he saw the baby. I . . . I want to give this one more try."

"You're insane."

"Maybe. But he's willing to follow my lead. I guess I want a chance to see if this will go anywhere. If it fails, then I have Matthew and my life is complete."

"Liar. Please be careful. I don't know if either of us could handle you going through another breakup like last time."

"I promise I will. If I decide that I want Eli again, he's going to have to work to prove himself to me."

He didn't need to see Meg's face to know she wasn't happy with him. "I better go. Josh wanted to watch a movie."

"Okay. I'll keep you in the loop."

Matthew flopped over onto his side, which was pretty much his indicator that he was out for the night now. Ignoring the ache in his back and the questions spinning in his brain, Devan got up and put his son to bed.

— CHAPTER — TEN

Eli knew what he was doing crossed all sorts of boundaries. It made him an asshole at best and a stalker at worst. Still, he knew Devan better than the man probably knew himself, which was why it wasn't too difficult to figure out what restaurant he would have suggested for a first date.

It was, in fact, where they'd gone on their own first date years ago.

The bar gave him perfect line of sight to watch Devan and the man who'd shown up twenty minutes ago. He was tall, dark-haired, and muscular—exactly the type of man who Devan always gravitated toward. Eli disliked him immediately.

Devan had his back to him, which made his spying easier. No doubt he would have spotted Eli within moments if he were facing the other way. And that would have caused a scene that he would have regretted.

The entire trip to the restaurant, Eli had tried to convince himself that this was only for his own peace of mind. Devan had the right to date whomever he wanted, and Eli certainly didn't have a say. But the thought of any man getting close to him made Eli want to punch something hard. Not exactly the expected reaction of a man who wanted nothing to do with Devan or his ideas of having a family.

He hoped seeing Devan on a date would be enough to help cull this crazy obsession that he was forming with his ex. It wasn't fair to Devan, and it was a distraction that Eli could ill afford right now. So he'd made a deal with himself—come in and check on Devan while he had one drink, and then he had to leave.

That had been two drinks ago.

Given that they weren't alcoholic, he couldn't claim the satisfaction of having a buzz.

The man sitting across from Devan was smiling and leaning forward, arms braced on the table. Their appetizers had arrived, though it seemed only Devan was eating them. The man's arms were waving around as though he was explaining something exciting, and Devan was nodding at regular intervals.

It didn't take Eli long to guess that whatever the man was saying, Devan was bored stiff. It was the same motion he'd use whenever someone cornered him at a party and he was trying to be polite. Eli had only been on the receiving end of that once during their second official date. He'd quickly changed the topic from fight schedules to current movies. Devan's relief had been obvious, and Eli never made that mistake again.

Eli had always been pretty good at reading others' tells, and that was Devan's big one. If they'd still been together, this would be about the time Devan would start to look around for him and give him *the look* to come rescue his ass. Eli would have gone over, wrapped his arm around Devan's shoulders, and whispered something dirty in his ear. That was normally enough to give whoever he'd been talking to a clear message that Devan was about to leave.

Too bad he couldn't do that tonight.

The bartender came over and wiped the bar in front of Eli. "Can I get you another club soda?" There was a hint of amusement in his voice. "Or would you like something else?"

"Another." Eli tossed down a twenty. "Keep the change."

The bartender snorted. "Coming up, big spender."

While Eli was distracted, Devan's meal had arrived. A salad from the look of it. Probably something overly healthy, knowing him. Devan was as lean and fit as he'd been three years ago; Eli would have fun putting him through his paces at the gym. He did look tired though; no doubt from having to be up with Matthew through the night. Teething sounded miserable for all involved.

As time went on, Devan's nods slowed in frequency and he started to lean back further in his chair. The man had no idea that he'd already lost Devan and continued to smile and chat away. There'd be no second date, which meant that there was one less man Eli had to worry about for competition. It was probably for the best if he left before Devan saw him. Being caught wouldn't bode well for his chances at making amends.

He got up, nodded to the bartender, and was about to go when he saw something that stopped him cold. The man had reached across the table and was holding Devan by the wrist. Eli could see the strain in Devan's body, trying to pull free without looking too obvious about it, but it clearly wasn't working.

The man's eyes were wider, and his body language was all wrong. His head was tilted down and his legs were spread wide. The man was leaning forward, far closer to Devan's personal space than he should have been.

Without thinking, Eli strode across the restaurant and stood beside the table. "Is there a problem here?" Devan's eyes were wide and his mouth was open as he stared up. Eli was only marginally aware of the reaction, as all of his attention was focused on the other man at the table. "Your date here doesn't seem to like your attention."

The man quickly let go of Devan's wrist. "What the hell is your problem?"

"My problem is that I was sitting at the bar enjoying a drink and I see a man physically restraining another person, someone who clearly doesn't want it." He turned to look at Devan now. "Unless I'm mistaken."

"Thank you for the wonderful meal." Devan stood and grabbed his jacket. "I'll ask the waiter to split the bill."

"Don't bother." Eli reached into his pocket and threw a fifty down. "That should cover it."

Devan's face was flushed. "Thanks."

It was only then that Eli realized they'd drawn the attention of most of the people within close proximity of the table. "Are you fine to get to your ride?"

"Yes. Thank you." Devan glanced around quickly before fleeing the restaurant.

Rage threatened to spill out of Eli. He needed to get the hell out of here and make sure that Devan was okay. Leaning in, he lowered his voice so that the man was the only one who would hear. "You better think twice before you grab anyone like that on a date again."

The man's eyes were so wide they looked to be bulging from his head. "I will."

Eli left, a smattering of light applause following him out. He doubted very much that anyone would have cheered him on if they realized the reason he'd actually been there.

He'd barely made it out the front door of the restaurant when Devan stepped in front of him. "What the actual fuck are you doing here?"

"Having a drink."

"You don't drink when you're training."

"It was club soda."

"You can buy that at the store."

"I wanted to stretch my legs." Eli's jaw clenched. He didn't want this to turn into a fight, because he'd never backed down from one. "I wasn't going to do anything."

Devan groaned. "But you did, Eli. You did."

"He grabbed you, was clearly making you uncomfortable. I would have stepped in to help any person in the same situation." Knowing it had been Devan, though, had pissed him off more than had it been a random stranger.

Devan closed his eyes, his breath visible in the cold November evening air. "I'm not *just* anyone. I can't do this." He turned and walked away.

Eli froze. Fuck, what the hell had he done? He started to follow Devan, wanting to grab him and make him understand his intentions. Devan was moving too quickly, and within moments he'd be out of reach forever.

"I'm sorry." Eli watched Devan stop. "I shouldn't have come."

Devan spun around. "No, you shouldn't have. I know things have been better between us the past few weeks, but don't think for a second that I trust you. You haven't done anything to earn that back. Not yet." The anger on his face bled away. "But thank you for your help."

The tension in Eli's chest relaxed. He took a step closer, happy when Devan didn't move. "How can I make it up to you?"

Devan took a few steps toward him. "You can give me my space when I need it. That means not following me on dates."

God, Eli didn't want Devan going out with anyone. He was Eli's to have, to love, to make love to. *His.*

But he wasn't.

"How about I do something to help you?" Eli closed the gap between them. Devan's cheeks were red from the cold, his lips cracked from where he'd been biting his bottom lip. "Something that will make you know that I can't interfere with your dates."

"What?"

It was a risk making this proposition. It went firmly against Rule 1. Still, it was the best way he could prove himself to Devan. "I can babysit Matthew for you."

"No."

Eli waited a beat. "I'll do it for free."

"No."

"Why not? You want to have a chance to date. You don't want me to get in your way. Can you honestly tell me that you will go out, that you'll date as much as you want, if you have to pay for a babysitter? I know you. You won't."

"Rule 1 was that you weren't going to be involved in his life. Or have you forgotten that already?"

"As a romantic interest to you or as a father figure to him. I'm only going to be a babysitter. Nothing more." He had no idea why he wanted to push this as much as he was. He didn't want a child, and he didn't want Devan dating. But he did want to make amends, and this was the best way he could think of to accomplish that. "You get the best of both worlds."

Devan chuckled. "You never give up, do you?"

"You know I don't."

"Let me think about it."

"I'll give up my date with you. You can go out with someone else, and I'll stay home with Matthew."

"Do you even know how to look after a baby? Change a diaper?"

A flutter of panic raced through him, but he pushed it away. "You can show me that."

"But I can't show you how to handle his crying."

Eli waved him away. "If I can survive getting beat up in the ring, I'm sure I can manage a little crying."

Devan rolled his eyes. "I'll think about it."

Eli leaned forward, close enough to kiss, but didn't. "Come on." His teasing tone earned him another smile. "Find some nice man to go with, bring Matthew to the gym, and have a good evening. I'll even clean your apartment."

Devan rolled his eyes. "Not you too."

"Dude, you're a slob."

"I said, 'I'll think about it.'"

"That's all I ask." Eli straightened, shoved his hands in his pockets, and nodded. "I'll let you get home."

He was moving toward the parking lot when Devan called out, "Thank you."

Eli waved and continued on, knowing that round one had gone to him.

The gym was busier tonight than it had been since Eli had started working out there. Nolan had taken to hiding in the office, which meant Zack constantly moved between making sure Nolan was okay and checking on the trainers. Eli couldn't imagine what it was like to have the kind of anxiety Nolan dealt with, but he was a strong dude.

It had been two days since Devan had promised to *think about it*, which was two days longer than Eli had wanted to wait. Instead, he focused his attention on training.

No matter what time Eli arrived at Ringside to work out, the bag he used was always available. Zack had teased him that everyone knew his routine, his preferences, and didn't want to be the one who ruined his chances to win the fight against Caulfield. He hadn't considered the option of training anyplace other than his gym in Montreal. He knew the guys there, he had his coach, everything to be successful. Here at Ringside it was only him, and that was terrifying. He had his routine, could push himself hard enough, but there wasn't anyone there to guide him, to call him out when he was projecting his punches.

Ringside was a great local gym, but it lacked most of what he needed for serious professional training. Weights and heavy bags could only do so much. What he really needed were a few opponents he could go toe to toe with in the ring, but there weren't many guys he felt comfortable sparring with.

The young guy who'd been mirroring his moves was back again. His form had improved considerably, and while he wasn't going to be winning fights anytime soon, he was at a point where Eli might be able to push him a bit while helping himself.

"Hey." Eli waited until the kid looked up. "Get a head guard and get in the ring."

The constant buzz of noise in the gym died down. The kid looked around for a moment before giving his head a shake. "Me?"

Eli raised an eyebrow. "Unless you want someone else to be my sparring partner."

He'd never seen a man move that quickly before in his life.

Eli yanked his shirt off and climbed into the ring. It felt good to have canvas under his feet, to be back in the place that had started him on this path years earlier. The kid came in a few minutes later, his head guard in place.

"Do you have a mouth guard?"

The kid smiled, the black plastic over his teeth.

"Good. You ever fought MMA style before?"

He shook his head.

"What's your name?"

"Kevin." It came out muddled, but Eli had no problem understanding it.

Eli grinned and slipped in his own mouth guard. "Well, Kevin, this will be an experience. Don't hold back. Keep your guard up. Kicks, punches, holds. You know, whatever."

He started light, needing to get a feel for not only Kevin's skill set, but also to make sure he was warmed up.

Jab, jab, cross, side kick.

Kevin stumbled back, but didn't drop his guard. He rounded his shoulders, stepped in, and led with a few jabs of his own. Eli barely felt the contact, but Kevin had great form. It took a few minutes and more than a few landed punches for Kevin to let go and really get into the sparring. Kevin landed a snap kick to Eli's chest, sending him back a few inches and pulling a cheer from the watching crowd.

"Lucky shot." Yeah, this felt good, right.

Sweat beaded on Eli's skin and threatened to run into his eyes as they traded blows. Kevin was letting his right guard drop, which was too tempting to resist. He moved in quickly and wrapped Kevin up, knocking him quickly to the canvas and landing a punch to the side of Kevin's head.

Kevin tapped out, and the crowd watching applauded.

Eli rolled off and helped the young guy to his feet. "You keep dropping your right guard. Work on that. I want you to up your weights as well. You can easily push an extra twenty on your legs and another ten for your arms. The bulk will help with your power, but make sure you're using your hips on those crosses."

Kevin spit out his mouth guard. "Thanks, Mr. McGovern."

He chuckled. "It's just Eli."

They touched fists, and Eli was ready to leave. One moment came the rush of being back in the ring, and the next the air was sucked from his lungs.

Caulfield stood in the front door, an entourage and several sports journalists standing around him. People had their phones out, and Eli had no doubt whatever this would turn out to be would end up on YouTube and Facebook the second they were done.

"McGovern!" Caulfield strutted into the gym. The crowds parted, giving them a clear view. "You training for the amateur league now?"

"Shit," Eli muttered. He made sure to stand at his full height, crossed his arms, and stared down from the ring. It was wrong for Caulfield to be here, to encroach on his haven. Zack and Nolan had worked too hard to build this place up, he'd be damned if he'd let this asshole tear it down. "What the hell are you doing here?"

"I'm checking out the competition." Caulfield jumped up onto the ring, holding the top rope, and swung around to face the crowd. "I wanted to see the king's new kingdom."

"Get the hell out of here."

"Scared I'm going to show you up in front of all your little friends?" He jumped over the top rope and landed beside Eli. "How about we have a go now? Show these punks how real men fight." In a blink, Caulfield yanked off his shirt and kicked off his shoes.

"What the fuck are you doing?" Eli got in his space.

"Stirring up some publicity." Caulfield lifted his chin. "You don't have a problem with that? Do you?"

And without warning, Caulfield shoved Eli hard.

Cheers and shouts filled the room as the press and Caulfield's entourage rushed the ring. Before Eli realized what was happening, Caulfield took a swing, and Eli's instincts kicked in. He rolled out of the way and quickly got back to his feet. "You need to stop."

"Why, McGovern? Scared I'm going to kick your ass?"

Sparring with Kevin was one thing, but going toe to toe with Caulfield was something he wasn't ready for. Eli kept his distance, dancing around and doing his best to stay outside Caulfield's reach. "You're that anxious for me to knock you out again? I'm sure I rattled your brain pretty good last time."

Caulfield took another swing at him, but Eli ducked away easily. "You were lucky. You should have stayed down when I connected."

"Nope. And I won't stay down this time either. I'd say you hit like a girl, but that's an insult to women."

What the holy hell was wrong with this guy? It was to no one's benefit for them to get into a fight now. Sure, the publicity might help spur ticket sales, but this was well beyond that. Out of the corner of his eye, Eli couldn't help but notice the sea of phones and faces following every move they were making.

"What the hell is going on?" Zack's booming voice filled the gym and drew Eli's attention at the wrong time.

As he turned his head to see his friend coming from the office to the ring, Caulfield took that moment to connect with a snap kick to Eli's chest. Unlike when Kevin hit him, this time Eli landed flat on his back.

"Get out of here!" Zack was in the ring and in Caulfield's face. "This is a private gym and not a fucking side show." He pointed to the entourage and press that were there as well. "Unless you have a membership or are signing up for one, I'm asking you to leave. Now."

Eli got to his feet, tamping down the physical pain to ensure no one would think he'd been hurt. He couldn't afford to appear weak, to show any hole that Caulfield could go back and examine and exploit during their fight.

Zack looked over his shoulder and nodded toward the office. "Nolan is in there with an ice pack. Go."

As he made his way to the office, the regular members were all nodding, giving him a thumbs-up as he went. If nothing else, he'd cemented his place here at Ringside.

Nolan was sitting in the chair behind the desk. His face was pale and his hands gripped the edge of the desk. "Who the hell was that insane man?"

"Jay Caulfield. The guy whose ass I kicked in the last fight."

"The one you're fighting in two weeks?" Nolan held out the ice pack. "Here."

"I'm fine."

"Oh good." Nolan placed it on the back of his neck. "Zack would have come out sooner, but my anxiety kicked in with the crowd and . . . yeah. Sorry."

In the few conversations he'd had with Zack, the subject of Nolan's past had come up only once. He didn't know exactly what had happened beyond him being in a car accident, but that was all that he needed to know. "It's good. You should take priority over my sorry ass."

Zack came into the office and closed the door. "Your sorry ass will be all over social media in about five minutes. If Caulfield wanted to drum up publicity, then he did exactly the right thing."

"Fucker." Eli rubbed his hand along the back of his neck. "At least the gym will get some publicity as well."

"Depending on who's doing the reading, that might not be a good thing. We'll have to wait and see." Zack came around the desk and put a hand on Nolan's shoulder. "You okay now?"

"Fine." The weak smile he gave Zack probably indicated otherwise.

"Take him home." Eli pushed away from the wall. "I'll stay until close and lock up for you."

Zack frowned. "Really? I figured you'd want to get out of here after what happened."

"Run back to my empty house and do what?" He shrugged. "I can use the ice pack here as well as there. Get out and the two of you go home."

Zack helped Nolan to his feet. "I owe you."

"Nope. Go."

He watched through the window as his friends left, wishing he had someone to be with like that.

No.

He'd fucked that up with Devan and had no right to pine for something that he'd carelessly thrown away. If nothing else, Caulfield reminded him, in the most painful way possible, that this was what he'd chosen over domestic tranquility. He'd wanted this life, this career, and there was no reason to regret it now.

Once everyone had gone back to their workouts, Eli left the office and ducked into the locker room. He fished his phone out of his gym bag and checked to see if Devan had contacted him.

Nothing.

He tossed the phone back and slammed the door shut. It was probably for the best. He didn't want to drag Devan and especially Matthew into this world. It was one of the reasons he'd left in the first place.

Ignoring the growing ache in his chest—it was probably from the kick anyway—Eli grabbed his things and headed for the shower.

CHAPTER ELEVEN

"Oh my God, Devan. Have you been on Facebook today?" Meg was through the door before Devan had finished opening it.

As per his normal Saturday morning routine, Devan had yet to get dressed and had been playing on the floor with Matthew. His sleep pants were frayed around the cuffs and the elastic band around his waist didn't hold anywhere as well as it had used to. It wasn't exactly the sort of thing he'd normally wear in front of anyone. Thankfully, Meg wasn't *anyone*.

"And good morning to you too." He made a beeline to the kitchen to get her a coffee, knowing she'd want one without her asking. "No, Mattie and I were playing and cuddling."

When he came back out into the living room, Meg had picked Matthew up and was plying his face with kisses. "Do it. I've got him."

He put her coffee down on the table and went in search for his phone. "If this is some weird political thing, I'm really not interested."

"This falls under sports. I figured you'd be more than interested."

Devan's heartbeat kicked up a notch. "Eli?" *Shit, where the hell was his phone?*

"I sent you a Messenger link. I wanted to be the one to let you know."

If Meg was here, that meant it couldn't be anything good and she was worried he'd freak out. He finally found his phone in the bathroom under one of Matthew's nightshirts. Meg's link was there, and it took only a second for it to load.

There was Eli, standing in a boxing ring staring down at some man Devan didn't recognize. The guy was clearly trying to bait Eli, but Devan could tell from the look on his face that he wasn't going to bite. Eli's skin glistened in the light, despite the somewhat grainy quality of the video. With his arms crossed, the muscles in his biceps flexed, as did his pecs.

Damn it, he really was a beautiful man to look at.

Devan hadn't really been paying attention to what the other guy had been saying, but when he jumped into the ring and ripped off his shirt, Devan knew what was going to happen. Eli ducked and weaved his way out of reach, but clearly wasn't expecting the kick. Devan gasped as Eli hit hard on the canvas.

God, why did he do that to himself? Put himself into positions where his body would be punished. The guy had clearly landed a cheap shot, but Eli surprisingly kept his temper in check. He'd always been good at that.

With his phone in hand, he wandered back out to the living room. Meg had put Matthew into his playpen and was now drinking her coffee. "I have to say, Eli is still looking good."

"Yeah." He pulled out the chair and sat beside her. "I'm actually worried about him."

"Why? Did he say something when you saw him? Trying to earn your sympathy, no doubt."

He loved Meg like a sister, but when she made her mind up about someone, it was hard to change her way of thinking.

"He didn't seem himself."

"How the hell would you know what that is anymore? It's not like he's been around." There was something off in her voice. Meg wasn't a harsh person, but there was an edge that wasn't normally there.

"Hon, what's wrong? And don't tell me it's about that video."

Meg blinked as unexpected tears rolled down her cheeks. "Josh and I had a fight. It's fine."

Clearly it wasn't. Devan pulled her in for a hug. "Is there anything I can do to help?"

She chuckled and wiped her tears as she moved away. "You can let me meddle in your life. It's better than mine at the moment."

"God, I couldn't stop you even if I wanted to." Meg and Josh had been happily married for nearly four years now. The timing of their fight brought back unhappy memories of his own. "Eli interrupted a date I had the other night."

"He *what*?"

"It was fine. Honestly, I was praying for someone to notice there was a problem, but that someone turned out to be Eli. I was trying to get away from my date, the guy turned out to be a major creep, grabbed my arm hard, and wouldn't let me leave."

"Well, I guess it's good that he was there for you."

"It was. But at the time I was so pissed at him, I walked away after we had a little fight. I haven't talked to him in days."

He hadn't known how to feel about the entire night. Eli had invaded his privacy, butted into a situation that he had no business being involved in. And yet Devan had been wishing someone would notice that he'd been trying to get away from his date. When the man had grabbed his wrist and squeezed, Devan had been genuinely scared for his safety.

When he'd looked up and seen Eli standing by the table, glaring down at his date, instead of anger, Devan had only felt relief. Eli had cared enough—albeit in his twisted-logic way—to make sure he was okay. It didn't excuse the stalking, but it certainly let him know that maybe there was hope. For what exactly, he wasn't sure.

"He apologized and said that if I wanted to date other men, then he would happily babysit Matthew for me. He was willing to give up the chance to go on a date with me if that would help." It had been a sweet offer, one that had brightened his mood.

Even if it went against Rule 1.

Rather than freak out the way he'd expected, Meg looked more than a little impressed. "That's interesting. I didn't think he'd want anything to do with Matthew."

"Me either. But I'm not sure it would be a good idea. I don't want Matthew getting attached and then being upset if he has to leave."

"Honey, Matthew wouldn't remember one way or the other. This is about you and Eli, nothing more." Meg looked over to where Matthew was playing with Mr. Fuzzy. "You have a good life with Mattie, but I know you're lonely. Eli screwed things up with you, and I'm the last person to push you in a direction you don't want to go. But maybe you should take him up on his offer to babysit. You get to go on some dates, and he'll get a small taste of what your life is like.

Not to mention that he might appreciate a place to hide out from the spotlight for a while."

"You're deviously logical. You know that, right?"

"I am." And for the first time since her arrival, Meg smiled. "It's my superpower."

She did have a point. Eli was usually all-in when it came to his training, but Devan remembered how much he needed his downtime as well. Not that Devan *needed* a babysitter—he had a perfectly good one already—but the chance to see Eli while still gaining a bit of freedom of his own, that was an opportunity too good to pass up. "I'll text him and see when he's free to come over."

Meg took a big sip of her coffee. "You'll also need to find a date. Someone who will make Eli jealous."

"I'm not going to throw that in his face. He's doing me a favor, and I'm trying to see if there's someone out there for me." Someone other than Eli.

"Is there someone who you've seen recently who you'd like to go out with again?"

Matthew gurgled and threw Mr. Fuzzy against the side of his playpen. Devan watched his beautiful boy playing and wondered what was the right decision. He'd spent some time on a couple of online dating sites the other night. While there were a number of good-looking men out there whose profile matched Devan's image of a perfect man, there'd always been something that had held him back. It wasn't their looks, or their bios, but rather he didn't feel that tug, the spark that had flared up the moment he'd laid eyes on Eli.

He'd never know if he didn't put himself out there and try. "I talked to a guy online a few times. His name is Pierce. We have a bunch of things in common. He might be a good option."

"Perfect! Ask him out for dinner. See if there's something there. Your relationship with Eli didn't happen overnight, a new relationship won't either."

Meg's phone chose that moment to buzz. She looked down at it for half a second before tossing it on the table. Devan didn't need to ask to know who the message was from. "Josh groveling yet?"

"Not yet. Just wondering where I'm at. Which means he's not angry any longer, but he's not sure what my current mood is."

"As if you'd be anywhere but here." No doubt, Devan's phone would start ringing soon enough if Meg kept giving Josh the cold shoulder. "What was the fight about?"

Meg's gaze drifted over to Matthew. "You know when I said I wasn't interested in having any kids of my own?"

Oh. "That's starting to change?" Despite Meg being his surrogate, he'd never thought she'd ever change her mind about starting her own family.

"Maybe. I don't know. Josh really doesn't want any, and he's always been up front about that. I didn't think I wanted any either."

Devan took her hand. "But?"

"But the other week when we watched Mattie for you when you were at the dentist, I don't know, something sort of clicked with me. I stayed up with him, and played on the floor with him. I know it's not all sunshine and roses having a baby. I know how hard it is on you being a single dad. But . . ." She gently shook her head. "I haven't been able to stop thinking about it. About having my own child to hold and sing to sleep. About them getting older and going trick-or-treating."

He'd been there, back when he and Eli were still together. Having a child had been the one thing that had driven him. "Speaking from experience, you need to talk this out with Josh. Seriously consider all of your options. It's stress on a relationship, even a solid one. But if you're not both on the same page . . ." He sighed. "If this is something you want, truly want, and he isn't willing to go there—"

"Then I might have to reconsider my relationship." Meg dropped her head to her hands. "I knew you were going to say that."

God, he didn't like to see her going through this, not after all she'd done for him. "I wish I could help. But this is something the two of you really need to work out. That said, I'm here for you, forever and always. No matter what."

He hugged her again. Why did life have to be so complicated about these things? All he'd ever wanted was a small family to love. That was it. He'd never had one of his own growing up. While he loved his foster parents, loved that they'd taken him into their home and treated him as one of their own, he couldn't help but feel like an outsider. When he'd met Eli, that had been something that they'd had in common. He'd always assumed it would be a strong enough foundation to cement their relationship.

He'd never been so wrong.

Meg sighed and got up from her chair. "I should probably go so you can make some phone calls. You need to get that date set up and the big man here is going to need a fresh diaper from the smell of him."

Damn, she was right. "What are you going to do?"

"A little retail therapy, maybe some Starbucks. Then I'll be ready to talk to Josh." She grabbed her coat. "You're right that I should probably give myself some time to think things through as well."

"It isn't a decision you can change your mind on." Matthew pulled himself up with the help of the playpen side and started yammering. "Because the little man keeps you busy. But Meg, I don't regret the decision, not even a little. Despite it making the days long and it costing me my marriage, I would make the same choice all over again."

He gave Meg a kiss on the cheek and saw her to the door. Once she'd left, he changed Matthew, grabbed his phone, and sat down to figure out who would be his next attempt at a date.

Eli had finished his shower after his latest workout at Ringside, when Grady came into the locker room. "There's the man I was looking for."

He hadn't spent much time with Grady, mostly because the other man was out looking for investors for the gym, or spending time flirting with Max. Another disgustingly cute couple. "What can I do for you, pretty boy?"

"You can totally do some social media promos using Ringside as your background." Grady leaned against the locker beside where Eli was changing. "That little video of Caulfield's has had Nolan swamped with membership applications and calls from the media about when you started training here."

Eli shouldn't have been surprised by that particular revelation, given how busy the gym had been today, but he was. He wasn't a main card fighter, not yet at least, so he'd never assumed he'd be that much of a draw. "And you want me to do more?"

"Look, I'm not your manager and I don't know what media constraints you're under. All I'm focused on is building Ringside up as much as possible." Grady ran his hand though his hair and shot Eli a smile that could melt hearts. "Can we film some of your training? Or if that's not good, maybe film you teaching someone? I saw you with that kid the other day, and you're really good at that."

He loved fighting, training, and being around the gyms, but Eli had never been a big fan of the media circus that came with the gig. Still, it wasn't a bad idea, and if it would help Zack and Ringside, then it was the least he could do. "Sure. I'll see what we can do, as long as it doesn't interfere with training."

Grady clapped his hands together. "Sweet. Thanks, man."

Eli's phone buzzed, and he pulled it from his locker.

I need a sitter 2morrow night. U free?

Grady chuckled. "I don't know if that was a booty call or not, but the look on your face is awesome."

Eli glared at him. "It's my ex. He needs a babysitter for his son."

"That's Devan, right? The cute guy from upstairs?"

"Yeah."

"I'm surprised he's your ex the way you were going at it. I felt bad for interrupting your little tête-à-tête. Max was shocked when I told him about you being with someone."

Eli had been beyond annoyed with that interruption. He'd wanted nothing more than to engage in a make out session that would have put a teenager to shame. But he knew that taking things too far, too fast with Devan would only end up with them walking away from one another. That was something that he wouldn't have. The spark that had always existed between them was still there, and the fact others could see it too gave Eli hope.

"I guess I better let you get to your babysitting duties." Grady pushed away from the lockers. "And don't forget about the social media stuff."

Eli waved him off, his mind already focused on Devan. *When and what time do you need me?*

2morrow night? If you're training, I'll get my regular sitter.

No way Eli was going to let that happen. *What time?*

7pm.

I'll be there.

Annoyance and jealousy were competing inside him to break free, but Eli knew he had no right. This had been what he'd wanted to do for Devan, to make up for stepping into his date the other night. It would also give him a break from being hounded at the gym, and being alone at his mom's house. Plus, Matthew was a damn cute baby.

He could make this work, and maybe Devan would see that he wasn't as horrible a person as he'd so far proven to be.

Besides, how hard could it be to look after an eleven-month-old?

= CHAPTER =
TWELVE

E li held Matthew in his arms, trying to determine exactly *what the hell that smell was* while wondering how it was possible for such a small being to cry nonstop for such a long period of time.

"Come, on dude. I just changed your diaper." Eli held him up, spun him around, and sniffed his ass again. "You did not crap yourself again."

When he spun Matthew back around, he was faced with a quivering mouth and watery eyes. "Da da da da."

"Your dad is out with some dude, little man. You're stuck with me." Eli hadn't felt this much like a rookie since the first time he stepped in the ring.

Matthew's lip stuck out further.

"Let's get you changed again. Then . . ." He looked around the room. "Then I have no fucking idea."

Devan had been surprised when Pierce had invited him to dinner at the CN Tower restaurant. Despite growing up in Toronto, he'd only ever been to the top of the tower for school trips. The restaurant was pricier than what he'd normally go for, but the view couldn't be beat. "This is amazing."

Pierce was in his thirties, with short cut black hair and eyes so blue they didn't look real. When he smiled, there was a sparkle to them that made his face light up. "It's been a while since I've eaten here. I forgot how nice it is at night."

They'd agreed to go dutch, so at least Devan wouldn't have to worry about an awkward bill exchange later. "I'm glad you suggested it. Normally I have my son with me, so I avoid places that are too fancy."

"His name's Matthew, right?" Pierce looked right at Devan, leaning forward slightly. "How old is he?"

"Eleven months. Almost a year." There was something about the way Pierce spoke that made Devan feel as though he were under a microscope. "Do you have kids?"

Ah, there was a bit of a chink in Pierce's armor. He shook his head, looking a little sad. "No. I, ah. My marriage was to a girl I met in university. We were good friends, but I hadn't figured out a few key things about myself."

"So you're bi?" Devan realized that might have sounded bitchy, and held up his hands. "Not that it matters to me. I was only curious."

Pierce shrugged. "It's fine. No, I'm gay. I was in denial for a long time. I only came out recently."

Devan couldn't imagine how difficult that must have been. Men like Pierce, and even Eli for that matter, felt the need to keep who they were hidden from the world. Devan was thankful every day that he hadn't been forced into a similar situation. "That must be a relief? Not having to hide?"

"It is. It gives me the pleasure of going out with a charming man such as yourself."

Devan's face heated. "Yeah, I'm not the charming one at the table."

Pierce chuckled. "Let's take a look at the drink list."

Dear God, how could so much crap come out of such a small body? Not only had Matthew filled his diaper, but it had gone up his back. Devan hadn't mentioned anything about giving Matthew a bath—like how to do it—but Eli was a smart man. He could figure this out.

Thankfully, the little man liked the water, which helped calm him down. By the time Eli was scrubbing him down, Matthew was giggling.

"You're a terror." Eli grinned and stuck out his tongue.

Matthew giggled again and stuck his own out.

The pain in Eli's back from leaning over the tub melted away as an unexpected warmth spread through him. This was the thing Devan had so desperately wanted, this genuine connection with another human being that wasn't beholden to anything. No wonder he'd fought so hard to have Matthew.

Eli blinked against the rush of tears. "Soap in my eye."

Matthew stuck his tongue out again.

Once the wine had been served, Devan let himself fall into a pleasant back and forth with Pierce. He was charming and easygoing to the point that they were both laughing like fools before their main course had arrived. Devan was relaxed and having a wonderful time. This was probably the best date he'd been on since before Eli had walked out on him.

"Whoa." Pierce put his fork down. "You okay?"

"Yes." Devan wiped his mouth on his napkin, hoping it would hide his embarrassment. "Why?"

"Have you ever been told that you don't have a poker face?" Pierce leaned back in his chair. "Seriously. Your entire face changed there for a second. What were you thinking?"

This wasn't exactly the best time to mention Eli, but Devan was a firm believer in getting all the crap on the table as soon as possible. "I was thinking about my ex, Eli."

"Sorry. Did things end badly for you?"

"He walked out on me after my friend miscarried our baby. He's currently babysitting my son for me."

Pierce blinked. "That's messed up."

Devan laughed. "Believe me, I'm well aware."

"So, you're on good terms. That's something at least."

"Do you mind if we don't talk about him? I don't want to put a damper on our evening." The truth of the matter was, he was having a hard enough time getting Eli out of his head as it was. He didn't need his current date to bring up emotions Devan certainly hadn't processed.

"Sure. How about we talk about what movie we should go to on our next date." Pierce leaned forward. "That is, if you want to go on another date."

Devan couldn't deny that he'd been having a good time. "Yeah, that might be nice."

Eli's body was used to working out, building his strength. He could go for hours in the gym, push himself to his limits in a fight. So why the hell was he so tired from playing with a toddler? "Okay, little man, what do you want to do now?"

Matthew was crawling around the living room, dragging Mr. Fuzzy as he went, babbling. What Eli needed was a bit of a break. He could do something to keep Matthew still for a while, then he could rest. There was a small bookcase in the corner of the apartment that held an assortment of children's books. Reading was good. He'd do a few stories, and then it would be time for Matthew to go to sleep.

"How about a book? Do you like books?" Eli leaned over and grabbed the first thing he saw. "Dr. Seuss. Kids like this shit, right?"

Matthew caught sight of what was in Eli's hand and squealed.

"Ah fuck."

Devan and Pierce talked for another half hour and paid for their meal. Pierce moved a bit closer to him as they went down the glass elevator that gave them an amazing view of Toronto. Devan turned to glance up at Pierce at the same time as Pierce looked down at him.

The brush of their lips could barely qualify as a kiss, but there was no mistaking the contact.

Devan blushed. "Sorry."

"I'm not." Pierce smiled. When the elevator doors opened and they stepped out onto the plaza, he turned to face Devan. "I did have a good time tonight. I'll give you a call in a day or two. We can see about that movie?"

"That sounds good."

Devan gave him a little wave before heading over to where the cabs waited. With each step he took, he couldn't help but turn over the brush of their lips. It should have been exciting, arousing. He'd done the same with Eli at the gym in the yoga studio before things had gotten hot and heavy. But the gentle kiss with Pierce hadn't stirred anything in him. Maybe it was simply too soon. Meg was right that his relationship with Eli hadn't begun overnight. He couldn't assume it would happen with anyone else that quickly either.

Lust though. He'd felt an undeniable attraction for Eli the moment their eyes had met.

No, he owed it to himself to see where this thing with Pierce could go. He hailed a taxi and headed home.

Devan moved down the hallway from the elevator toward his apartment with a sense of excitement. He'd had a decent date, and hadn't gotten a call or text from Eli. Hopefully that meant he'd had no trouble getting Matthew in bed. It always amazed him how much he missed their bedtime routine on the odd night when he wasn't home to do it.

He fished his keys out of his pocket and slid open the apartment dead bolt. He'd told Eli that he'd be home around nine, so he would no doubt be surprised to see him a half hour earlier. The apartment was quiet except for the sounds of one of Matthew's Baby Mozart DVDs. Not sure what he was walking into, Devan crept as quietly as he could into the living room. The laundry basket of unfolded baby clothes and towels had been put away. The bevy of toys normally strewn around the floor had all been picked up and put in the toy box. As he stepped fully into the room, he was greeted with a sight he'd never imagined he would see.

Eli was fast asleep on the couch with Matthew cuddled to his chest.

In that instant, Devan's heart exploded with emotions he didn't dare label.

This was what he'd always wanted. Exactly this. His husband and his son being together in the home that he and Eli had tried to make work since they first got married.

Eli must have sensed his presence, because in a moment he was moving, yawning and slowly shifting to look up at him. "Hey."

"Did he wear you out?"

Eli blinked several times before carefully adjusting Matthew. "I don't know how you do this."

Devan grinned as he scooped Matthew up. "I'll put him to bed."

Holding his son to his nose, he breathed in the normal scent of baby powder and fresh diaper. This time the smell of Eli's soap mingled with it, which sent a shiver through him. Matthew never woke as he placed in him his crib. With any luck, he'd sleep through the night and Devan would get a decent night's sleep.

When he got back out into the living room, he was surprised to see Eli still sitting on the couch. Not that he was in any hurry to rush him out the door, but he figured after an hour and a half of watching an eleven-month-old, he'd be ready to leave.

"How was he?" Devan fell into the chair opposite Eli, taking advantage of the opportunity to really look at him.

"When he realized that I'd read books to him, he got excited. He cried whenever I tried to stop. He didn't rest until twenty minutes ago. That movie thing helped distract him so I could take a break. I guess I fell asleep too."

"Yes, I should have warned you about the book thing. What one did he fixate on tonight?"

"*The Cat in the Hat*." Eli's scowl told him all he needed to know about what he thought of Dr. Seuss.

"Well there are worse things that could have happened."

Eli leaned forward, his hands on his knees. "How was the date?" There wasn't any underlying edge to his question, more general curiosity.

"It was okay."

Eli cocked an eyebrow. "Only okay?"

Because he wasn't you. "It was great. Pierce was nice enough, but he's only recently out, and I'm not sure he knows what he's looking for yet. We're probably going on another date though."

Eli nodded. "I'm glad." He didn't sound the least bit pleased.

"If nothing else, I can finally say that I had a chance to eat at the CN Tower."

"That sounds like fun." Eli got up, and Devan assumed that that was it, he'd be out the door. Instead, he walked over to where Devan sat and held out his hand. "Come here?"

It was strange how natural it felt to slide his hand into Eli's. To let himself be tugged to his feet and have Eli's hand fall to his waist. When they started swaying together, Devan laughed. "Are we dancing to Baby Mozart?"

"Your date ended early. You look like you weren't ready to come home."

Words fell away, and Devan enjoyed the contact between them. Whenever they touched, Devan's body zinged with arousal. The blood pounded harder through his body, and his cock inconveniently took notice. God, why the hell hadn't he responded this way to Pierce? He was attractive, smart, and funny; Devan had enjoyed their night and really did want to go out with him again. But despite their fledgling attraction, there hadn't been the same rush of instant connection he'd felt with Eli.

Instead of fighting against his turbulent emotions, he stepped closer and laid his head on Eli's shoulder. "This is nice."

There'd never been anything soft about Eli—at least, it had seemed that way until Devan had gotten to know him. Whenever they'd been in bed together, Devan had marveled at how strong he was. Time hadn't changed that aspect of him, but that gentleness was still there, the thing that had drawn Devan to him in the first place. It was as unsettling as it was reassuring.

"Anything new happen on the Caulfield front today?"

Eli grunted. "Stephan called me a few hours ago and read me the riot act. He also said that Caulfield has been warned by the league, so I don't think we'll have any more unsanctioned interactions before the fight. His scheme worked though. Stephan said tickets for the match are sold out."

A sold-out fight no doubt meant better pay-per-view ratings. The league would be happy, and Eli would no doubt move up another notch in their eyes. "Congratulations. Are you ready for the match? How's the training been?"

"Can we not talk about the fight? I'm enjoying my night off."

Eli wasn't normally one to deflect when it came to talking about his job, so Devan didn't want to push. "Night off? So babysitting was that easy, eh?"

"Hell no. Like I said, I don't know how you do it all the time without anyone to help you."

"Well, I'd always hoped there would be someone else around." When Eli didn't say anything else, Devan pulled back. "Sorry. I didn't mean that as a dig against you."

Eli looked at him, but Devan couldn't read what he was thinking.

Yeah, he'd had enough confusion in one night. "Look, maybe you should go. I really appreciate you watching Matthew for me. Thank you for giving me a night off."

They stood there looking at one another, gazes locked. Devan's stomach churned, and he couldn't help but wipe his palms against the sides of his thighs. Eli didn't say a word, he simply closed the gap again. He reached up and cupped Devan's face. Unlike at Ringside, Devan didn't turn his face away, didn't try to avoid the inevitable kiss.

With his eyes closed, Devan parted his lips as Eli lowered his head. The first brush of their mouths together sent a chill through Devan. Memories he'd tried to bury for years now flooded his mind. His cock grew stiff as their bodies pressed against each other. Eli moaned so faintly, Devan wasn't sure he'd actually made the noise. Yes, *this* was what he'd wanted: the flare of want and need that he couldn't adequately describe to anyone. The passion that haunted his dreams.

The kiss deepened, as Devan ran his hands along Eli's arms, up his back. Muscles seemingly made of steel flexed beneath his touch. Eli walked them backward until the edge of the couch banged against their legs.

Devan moved with Eli as they sat down. Their kiss had grown more passionate, harder, more desperate. He didn't want to think about what they were doing, if it was a good idea or not. For the first time in forever, he didn't worry about Matthew and if he was going to be okay. The only thing that mattered was him and Eli, here together again.

The material of his dress shirt stretched as he leaned back and Eli's large body covered him. The angle and pressure made his cock strain in his pants. God, he wanted to be naked, to feel Eli on him, in him. He pulled at Eli's T-shirt, trying to wrestle it over his head while refusing to break their kiss. Once Eli knew what he wanted, he moved back, eyes dark and lips wet, and yanked his shirt off. "You. Unbutton your shirt."

Devan sighed and did as he was told. When he wasn't done as fast as Eli would have liked, he reached down and yanked the shirt apart, sending the remaining buttons flying every which way.

"Jesus." He slid the shirt from his arms. "I'll never find all those again. Matthew will eat them."

"I'll vacuum them up later." Eli went to work on the fly of Devan's pants. His large fingers easily found Devan's straining cock and gave it a hard squeeze. "There you are."

Devan's body seized up, refused to move or risk breaking this unbelievable spell that they'd fallen under. The feeling of Eli on him, touching him, was more than he could handle.

"You're hard as a rock. How long has it been?"

Devan swallowed. "I jerk off whenever I can."

"I mean with a man. How long?"

God, he didn't want to admit this. He turned his head, but Eli reached up with his free hand and grabbed his chin, forcing Devan to look him in the eye. "How long?"

"You. You were the last man I fucked."

Without letting go, Eli leaned closer. "Say that again."

Devan moaned. "You were the last man I fucked."

"Good." Eli freed him, shifted down Devan's body, and pulled his cock from his pants. "I'm going to make you scream."

The last time Devan had felt a hot mouth on his cock was over three years ago. Eli had been pumped up from a training session and needed to burn off some energy. He'd fallen to his knees in the kitchen, took Devan's cock out and sucked him until he came. It had been fast and immensely satisfying. That was the night before Meg had miscarried for the second time.

There wasn't the same urgency tonight, but the frantic energy was simmering below the surface. Eli licked up the length of his shaft, taking a moment to tease the tip of his cock with his tongue. Devan clutched at the cushions, praying that nothing would happen to stop this. Eli fisted his cock and began to stroke it as he worked the tip with his mouth. He'd always known exactly how to get Devan off, where to touch him and how hard to press. Given how long it had been since he'd last done this, Devan was terrified he'd come too quickly and it would be over.

"You're shaking." Eli ran his free hand across Devan's stomach, teasing the rim of his belly button. "Close?"

"Yes." Devan squeezed his eyes shut. "Please."

"That's something I forgot. You love to beg me in bed." He slowed his strokes until they were so painfully slow, Devan wanted to cry. "Say it again."

"Please." His voice was barely a whisper. "*Please*, Eli."

"That's my boy. What I like to hear." He lowered his head to Devan's cock once more and began to suck in earnest.

Muscles he'd lost control of shook harder than he thought possible. Heat from his balls spread through his lower body until it reached his lungs, making it difficult to breathe. There were no thoughts, no emotions, nothing but the surge of pleasure as his orgasm exploded. He started to cry out, but Eli reached up and covered his mouth with one hand. Devan bit down on the fleshy heel, knowing it was the only way to keep from screaming.

As the waves of his orgasm subsided and he regained the ability to think once more, he placed a kiss to the part of Eli's hand he'd no doubt hurt. "Sorry."

"Didn't want you to wake the baby." Come had slipped from Eli's mouth, a light sheen glistening on his lips and chin. "Forgot how good you taste."

Devan thumped his head back on the cushion. "Killing me." He didn't want this to be over. Neither the past nor the future mattered now, only this moment. "You next."

Eli didn't move immediately, which was completely unlike him when it came to sex. "I don't think I should."

"Why? Are you all right?" Just because Devan hadn't been with anyone else over the years, he hadn't assumed Eli was living the life of a monk. Still, if Eli had some sort of disease, then this was going to change a few things.

"I'm fine. I . . . don't deserve to be with you."

No, no, no, Devan did *not* want reality to kick in. Not yet. "Do you have a condom?"

"In my wallet."

"Get it."

"No."

Devan huffed. "Fine, then." Devan pushed at Eli until he was sitting on the couch. Ignoring the way he stared down at him, Devan opened up Eli's pants. "There's nothing wrong with me wanting to do this."

He wasn't exactly sure who he was reassuring.

The smell of Eli's arousal hit Devan hard as he freed the cock. It made his mouth water and his heart pound. The tip of Eli's cock was purple and leaking, which Devan knew meant he wouldn't last long. He forced his other hand into Eli's jogging pants and easily cupped Eli's balls as he took his first taste.

Eli groaned, his hand sliding into Devan's hair before fisting it. "Shit."

It only took a few moments for him to fall into the rhythm he knew always worked. Down, up with a teasing flick of his tongue across the sensitive cockhead. Over and over he moved as he became reacquainted with the delicious sounds Eli made.

"So hot when you suck me like that. I'd forgotten." Eli rubbed a thumb along Devan's temple and brushed his hair from his face.

Devan hummed, increasing the suction, and tugged lightly on Eli's balls. Ah, there it was, the little catch of breath that signaled Eli was close to coming. Keeping the pace exactly as it was, Devan did his best to memorize every second of this. He didn't know if it would ever happen again.

Eli tensed as the first splash of come covered Devan's tongue. It was bitter and wonderful, almost exactly as he remembered it being. Eli's body shook, his hard muscles quivering as he bit back his cries of pleasure. Devan waited as long as he could before pulling away. He leaned back against the couch and simply looked at Eli.

It didn't take long for Eli to regain his wits and crack open an eye to look at him. "Hi."

"Hi." Devan smiled. "So, that happened."

Eli closed his eye again. "It did."

There had always been these moments of silence between them. They'd never been uncomfortable or awkward. Devan had actually enjoyed them. Tonight though, the longer that they sat here, the more Devan began to wonder if this had all been a terrible mistake.

"What are you thinking about?" Eli's voice startled him.

"About us. This." Devan played with the frayed thread that used to hold one of his buttons. "We probably shouldn't have done this."

"Maybe not." Eli sat up, pushing his softening cock back into his pants. "We were always good together in bed."

That had been the easy part of their relationship. The reassurance of knowing that regardless of what had happened in the day, at night it was only the two of them together. Too bad the rest of their lives had gotten so complicated. "I went and saw about the paternity test kit the other day."

Eli sat up straighter. "And?"

"They were actually out of kits but should have more in a day or two." He'd put off going to the clinic for days until he couldn't any longer. While he didn't think Eli would try to take Matthew from him if Eli turned out to be the father, Devan wasn't sure how either of them would feel about it.

"I need to be here, right?"

Devan nodded. "I think they need samples from both of us. We have our workout tomorrow, and then I have a date tomorrow night with Pierce. Why don't we get together the day after to do it? I should have the kit by then"

"Sounds good." Eli grabbed his shirt and got to his feet. "I'd better let you get to bed."

Devan watched as Eli pulled his shirt back on and straightened his pants. In a few seconds, he looked as though nothing had happened. "I don't know what tonight means. I still plan to go on another date with Pierce."

Rather than look annoyed, there was a sparkle in Eli's eyes that Devan couldn't label. "That's fine. I want you to know for certain."

"Know what for certain?"

Eli smiled. "I'll see you at the gym tomorrow for your first workout." Then he left.

CHAPTER THIRTEEN

Devan felt out of place in his jogging pants and microfiber T-shirt standing in front of a weight bag. At least he thought that was what it was called. Eli had put some small fingerless gloves on his hands, hopefully to soften the contact he was supposed to be making.

Lord, he was so not a boxer.

"Okay, widen your stance, left leg forward." Eli came up behind him and kicked his right foot back a few extra inches. "There. That's better."

They'd drawn lots of attention from the other members of the gym. Apparently, it was a big deal to be trained by Eli, and Devan was clearly not worthy of such an honor. He did his best to ignore the other patrons and concentrated on the spot Eli had pointed to. "Now what?"

"I want you to punch it with your right hand. Try and turn your hips with the punch. That gives you power."

Devan brought up his guard, lowered his chin, and punched the spot on the bag. "Oh my God, ouch."

Eli snorted. "Dude, that was pathetic."

"I did what you said to." God, now he was *whining*. "Let me try again."

"Remember to shift your hips." Eli came up behind him and put his hands on his sides. "I know you're good at that when you need to."

Devan's face went beat red. "Asshole."

"Punch the bag."

Devan did and, with Eli's help, moved his whole body. The bag jerked from the contact, and Devan grinned. "That's better."

When Eli pulled away, he immediately missed his closeness. "Do that again fifteen times. Get your whole body into it as much as possible." As Devan punched, Eli walked around him, watching. "You and Pierce all set for your date?"

"We are." He'd spoken to him this morning. Pierce had texted to thank him again for dinner and sent a link to a movie that was playing at the TIFF Lightbox. "We're going to a foreign film festival."

"Glad he's taking one for the team." Eli drew closer. "Switch your stance. Do the same thing on your left side. I never could understand why you like those films so much."

"I remember." Devan used to tease Eli into coming with him to those movies. They normally would spend the movie annoying one another, before going to the bar for drinks.

"Do you need me to babysit Matthew again?"

"I didn't want to presume. Aren't you crazy busy training right now?"

"Keep your guard up. An opponent would punch you in the nose. I don't mind. It will give me a chance to rest up."

"Sure, as long as you don't mind." Devan did his very best not to think about what had happened between them after the last time Eli had babysat. "Tonight at six."

"I'll be there." Eli stopped beside him. "Good. Now I want you to get some weights. We're going to be doing dead lifts and squats."

Devan groaned. "Why did I agree to this?"

Eli shrugged. "I'm the best money can't buy. Now move."

He'd forgotten how much fun it was to be with Eli, to spend time with him, especially if they were doing something that wasn't exactly designed to be so. Pushing those thoughts aside, he went in search of the weights and hoped he'd still be able to move tomorrow.

Pierce folded his jacket on his lap as they got settled in their seats for the movie. "I heard that this movie is probably going to be up for an Oscar."

"I was doing some reading today on it. It sounds amazing." Devan winced as he shifted in his seat. No matter how hard he tried, he couldn't get comfortable.

Pierce watched him for a few minutes before shaking his head and chuckling. "Are you okay?"

"I started a new workout this morning. My trainer was an unrelenting beast."

"They can be the best and worst sort of people. I had a trainer once, a small twentysomething woman. She was the meanest person in the world, but damn if I didn't look good."

"Eli made me do these squat, burpee things that made me want to cry. I was cursing him after three and couldn't finish the second set." His ass and stomach still hurt, and so not for a pleasant sexual reason.

Pierce frowned, turning more in his seat to face him. "Eli? As in your ex who is also your babysitter?"

It took a second for Devan to realize that there was something off in Pierce's tone. "Yes. It's not like that. He's an MMA fighter, and he's getting ready for a match at the Air Canada Centre. I'm taking advantage of his skills while he's around."

Devan hadn't wanted to think about what would happen when the match was over and Eli had no reason to stay in Toronto any longer. He'd tried his hardest to keep his emotions regulated, indifferent, but every moment he spent with Eli made that increasingly difficult.

"Your ex is an MMA fighter. Who trains you and watches your kid." Pierce turned in his seat and faced the front. "What are you doing here with me?"

He hadn't realized how any of that sounded until he'd heard it parroted back to him. "I'm sorry. It's not like you think. I hadn't spoken to him until a few weeks past."

"It doesn't sound like you two are separated. If anything, if sounds as though he's trying to win you back." Pierce looked down at his jacket and fingered the fringe. "It's fine, you know. If you are still interested in him."

The normal thing for Devan to do in this moment was to argue with Pierce, to deny that there was any attraction at all, that *Dear God, he broke my heart, and I have no interest in that bastard ever again.* A regular person might go so far as to make some grand gesture, to prove to Pierce that he really wanted to be here with him and not back home with Eli and Matthew.

Leaning over, he turned Pierce's face and kissed him. He poured every ounce of emotion he could muster as he explored Pierce. The kiss was deep, sweet, and ended in a natural way that rarely seemed to happen anywhere but in the movies. Pierce was exactly the type of man that he *should* fall in love with. He was Eli's opposite in so many ways, exactly the right person to help him get over Eli and move on with his life.

But, after they pulled apart, Devan had a startling realization.

He didn't feel the same about Pierce as he did about Eli.

There was no passion, no spark, no bone-melting desire like what flooded Devan every time Eli came near him. Sure, they laughed and had a great time, but he had the same feelings when he was with Meg and they were watching a movie. Maybe something was wrong with Devan that prevented him from wanting anyone other than Eli? He could only guess.

Pierce must have sensed his confusion. "You know, I really do like you. But I don't think things are going to work between us."

Devan sat back in his seat. "I'm sorry."

"Hey, these things don't always work. I'd like to still be friends. I don't know a lot of people in the gay community yet. It would be nice to hang out, maybe talk about dates. Or not, if you think that will be awkward."

"God, no. I'd love that. I don't have anywhere near enough friends in my life." There was something right about keeping Pierce in his life, even if they didn't become romantically involved. "It will be nice to have someone to come to these movies with me. Eli hated them."

"He doesn't exactly sound like the art-house type." Pierce looked over at him. "You're okay, though? He's not pressuring you to take him back?"

"No. If anything, he's been a model gentleman."

"I know we don't know each other very well, but can I offer a piece of advice? Don't let him back in too quickly. Not because he'll be bad for you or anything like that. Just . . . he needs to make sure that the reason that drove him away in the first place has been resolved. Speaking as a man who took a long time to confront his secret, some of us would rather hide than face the pain of what the truth means."

The lights dimmed, cutting off the rest of their conversation and leaving Devan with his thoughts.

CHAPTER FOURTEEN

Eli was finishing up his last set of weighted leg squats when Nolan came over to him. "Hi. Sorry to interrupt."

He set the weights back on the rack. "It's fine. I can take a minute to recover. What's up?"

He and Nolan didn't speak much, because despite being in the same building, their paths didn't cross often. Maybe Zack had told him about what he'd done to Devan, and Nolan simply didn't want anything to do with him. Eli wouldn't blame him if that was the case. He hadn't forgiven himself yet.

"You had a message from some guy named Stephan."

"He's my manager."

"That's what he said, but I didn't want to take the chance that he was lying." Nolan's blush was cute. "He wanted to let you know that he's coming to the gym tomorrow, and he's bringing someone named Andrew with him?"

Eli groaned. "I guess that means my training is about to get serious."

"Ah. Well, he said he texted you the details of a press conference you're going to have soon. But he wanted to call because you've apparently been avoiding him."

Had he? Sure, he hadn't spoken to Stephan daily, but he was training, and his manager didn't tend to care about the details of his weight routine or diet. Then again, he'd been more than a little preoccupied by Devan and Matthew. "That sounds like something I'd do."

"I heard that about you." Nolan's eyes opened wide and his blush deepened. "Oh my God, I'm sorry."

Eli was too amused to be annoyed. "It's fine. Zack filled you in, I presume."

"He came home really angry one night and being more than a bit unreasonable." Nolan shrugged. "I have ways of making him talk."

Eli chuckled. "I have no doubt that you do."

Nolan stepped closer. "Did you sign the divorce papers?"

"I did."

"So, your ex is free now." Nolan nodded. "That's good."

Eli reached over and picked up more weights and started doing curls. "He has a son. Matthew. There's a chance that he's mine."

Nolan looked at him through the mirror. "I don't want to know how that's possible."

"It's a long story. I'm going over to his place tonight to do the paternity test so we know for certain. It will take a few days for us to get the results, but then we'll know."

Nolan cocked his head to the side, and for a moment, Eli thought he might be looking straight through him. "Do you think he's yours?"

Of all the questions that Eli had been asking himself, that was the one that had kept him up at night. "Yeah, I think he might be."

"What are you going to do if he is? I mean, are you going to ask for dual custody?"

"No. Matthew is Devan's and I wouldn't do anything to separate them." It had become obvious the more time he spent with Devan and Matthew that there was no way he'd do anything to get between them. He might have to leave Toronto once the fight was over and his mom's house was finally fixed up, but he'd be sure to offer whatever support he could to Devan. If that meant little more than having the occasional phone call when Devan was having a bad day, or coming to Toronto occasionally to spend time with them, then that was what he'd do.

"Then why do you need to know so bad? It was my understanding that you didn't want children, so why would knowing that he was yours make any difference?"

Eli stopped moving and really looked at Nolan. "I don't know." That was a lie. He wanted to know if there was a permanent connection between him and Devan. To know if Matthew was going to be a bridge that might bring the two of them back together.

"I don't know you well enough to offer any sort of advice. The thought of kids freaks me out more than I'd like to admit. I guess if knowing if Matthew is yours or not is so important to you, then maybe there is more to what you want than you're willing to admit."

Nolan handed him the paper with the message printed on it and went back to the office.

The time Eli'd spent with Matthew over the past few days had impacted him more than he'd realized. It had been fun, relaxing in a way that Devan probably wouldn't understand. Or maybe he would. The entire situation had been a revelation to Eli. The normalcy that he'd craved as a teen, and had run away from three years ago, was soothing to him. Matthew didn't want him to hide who he was, didn't care if he was the top fighter in the world, or if he was going to earn enough money. All he wanted was a clean diaper, a full belly, and Mr. Fuzzy.

The long nights when he couldn't sleep, normally a day or two before a fight, he used to lie in his bed and wonder what things would have been like if he'd stayed with Devan, if he'd been brave enough to go through the emotional rollercoaster of another pregnancy. Seeing Meg lying in that hospital bed, her pale face streaked with tears, had broken his heart. Devan was the one who was far more resilient when it came to emotional matters. Eli wasn't.

It had been easier to say that he didn't want children than to admit he couldn't bear the thought of going through another miscarriage.

He didn't know what kind of man that made him.

Eli pushed himself through the last set, sweat pouring down his face and chest. He was about to put his weights down, when movement in the mirror caught his attention. Devan came into the gym with Matthew propped on his hip.

"He's not supposed to be here today." Eli turned around, grabbing his towel to dry off, and waved at Devan. "I thought I was coming over after supper?"

Matthew smiled at him and waved his arms as though he wanted Eli to hold him. Eli didn't smile back, but stuck out his tongue, which drew a giggle from Matthew.

Devan rolled his eyes. "That's where he learned that from. Thanks."

"My job as your babysitter is to care for and corrupt your child."

"And yes, still on for tonight. My babysitter got sick, so I had to come home early. Then I thought I'd come down and see how you were doing with your training." Devan's gaze traveled down Eli's body. "Still pushing yourself."

"Always."

Eli was about to say something else, when Zack strode over. "Now, I know we're looking for youth members, but he might still be a bit young for Ringside." Zack smiled down at Matthew. "Aren't you a handsome fella."

"I have a feeling he'll be a heartbreaker when he gets older." Devan shifted Matthew to his other hip. "I was in the area and thought I'd say hello."

As always when Devan came around, they'd gathered a few curious onlookers, those no doubt who'd heard the rumors about Eli's sexuality. He hated not feeling like he could be honest about who he was, but there wasn't that sort of freedom yet in the sport. Devan swayed closer to him, and for a moment, Eli thought he might lean in and give him a kiss.

"Hey." Eli stepped away a bit too quickly. "Why don't you let me get cleaned up and then we can go talk?"

Devan looked at him, clearly confused. "Sure. That sounds great."

A few people turned their backs on them, but Eli couldn't help but think that they were still listening. "I'll be back in a few minutes."

He showered and changed in record time. When he came out, Nolan and Grady had joined the group. Grady had taken Matthew and was spinning him around, making him squeal. "And the airplane goes *weeee.*"

Eli paused, his gaze falling on Devan's face. He was grinning, his hazel eyes sparkling, an expression of joy that made him look lighter. That was the Devan he remembered, the man who'd quietly seduced him over a few weeks, who laughed when they were in bed and cried at romantic movies.

Damn it, he should never have walked away.

Realization three years too late, asshole.

He cleared his throat as he approached. "I'm all set."

Grady pouted. "Don't take the baby from me. I love the baby."

Devan chuckled. "I'll add you to the list of potential babysitters."

"Oh, maybe I can get Max to come too. We should totally have a kid to spoil." Grady's grin widened. "Poor Max."

Eli shook his head and picked the diaper bag and car seat off the floor where Devan had set them. "We better head out."

Devan took Matthew, and they waved to the group as they left. Eli didn't say anything until they were half a block from the gym. "Sorry about pulling away in there."

"It's fine. I forgot for a second that not everyone knows. I've gotten used to being closer to you there . . . physically . . . I mean because of the training." Devan huffed. "I'll keep my distance."

"I don't mind." He really didn't. Seeing Devan and Matthew had brought him unexpected joy. He should have smiled, laughed, scooped Matthew up and spun him around the way Grady had. But that fear of screwing up again, of knowing he wasn't the type of man who Devan needed as a partner, was enough to quash all of those emotions.

"Still, I'll be more careful next time."

"My car is over here." It only took Devan a few minutes to install the car seat in the back. Eli held Matthew as he watched. This was the life he'd given up, this normalcy that he'd never truly had as a kid. Matthew reached up and grabbed his nose. Eli stuck his tongue out, which drew another giggle.

"All set." Devan started to reach for Matthew and stopped. "Want to do it?"

"Sure." He set Matthew into the seat, but was momentarily confused by the buckles. "Shit, there's a lot of them."

"Keeps him safe."

It took a minute, but Eli eventually figured it out. "There you go."

Matthew stuck his tongue out in agreement.

When he stood up and closed the door, Devan was looking at him, grinning. "Not bad for a rookie." In a blink, he leaned up and placed a kiss on Eli's cheek. "That's what I wanted to do back at the gym."

That was a tease, something that Eli could handle. With a quick look around to make sure no one was paying attention to them, he cupped the back of Devan's head and kissed him. It wasn't as frantic as what they'd shared in Devan's apartment the other night, but Eli poured every drop of longing into it.

Devan's breath caught, and the look in his eyes was more than enough to reassure Eli that the feeling was mutual. "What was that for?"

"That's what *I* wanted to do back at the gym." He pressed his body against Devan. "I'm sorry I couldn't."

Devan looked away. "I wouldn't want you to get into trouble."

"I don't care. It was worth it." Eli took his hand. "Let me get you two home so we can do this test."

Devan nodded and got into the car. "What are we going to do once we know?"

"I'm not sure." But he had a few days to figure it out.

CHAPTER FIFTEEN

Devan put Matthew in his highchair and set the bowl of baby cereal in front of him. It had been a few days since he'd last seen Eli, since they'd taken a cheek swab and provided samples for the lab to test. Devan had taken the kit into the clinic and paid the fee on his way to work the next morning. The results should be in on Tuesday, which only gave him a few more days to ponder what exactly knowing who Matthew's biological father was would mean.

Eli kept insisting that he had no intention of trying to take Matthew from him. He simply wanted to know if he was the father. Devan believed him, but that didn't make this process any less nerve-racking. If it turned out that Eli was Matthew's biological parent, Devan had to make a decision whether he wanted to offer Eli a place in their lives or not.

After thinking about their time together, about Eli babysitting, their workout sessions, for the first time since Eli had materialized back into his life, Devan had hope that maybe things might work out between them. It really wouldn't be that bad if Eli was around, able to spend time with Matthew. He'd clearly become quite taken with Matthew, which was something Devan wouldn't have ever guessed.

Matthew was being surprisingly cooperative this morning, eating most of his breakfast while making minimal mess. Devan was happy to have today off from work. Friday mornings when he was around, he'd take Matthew to the Stars and Strollers movie morning. There were a few good movies out, and it was the only way he normally got to see anything.

"Okay, dude. Time to get you changed, and then we can go."

He was nearly finished packing up the diaper bag when there was a knock on his door. No one had buzzed up, which meant it was probably one of his neighbors, or possibly the superintendent. "Just a second."

Devan knew better than to open the door without checking who it was. But he'd been so fixated on leaving that he didn't think. "Hello?"

The man who stood there didn't look familiar, which meant someone had either buzzed him into the building without knowing who it was, or he'd snuck in. He wore a ball hat, jeans, and a heavy leather jacket. He was a few inches shorter than Devan, but appeared to be far more muscular. "Hi. You live here, yes?"

"May I ask what this is about?"

"Sorry. My name is Jason Earl. I saw you down at Ringside the other day with Eli McGovern."

God, this guy was a groupie. "I'm sorry, whatever it is you want, I can't help you."

"That's fine, I don't actually need anything. I wanted to confirm that you're the man who was at the gym the other day. The one with the baby." There was something about the way Jason spoke that set alarms off in Devan's head.

"You need to leave. This is a secure building, and I'm going to call the building supervisor."

He tried to shut the door, but Jason put his foot in the way. "I was curious who you are to Eli. Friend? Family? Boyfriend? Lover? Is the baby Eli's?"

Devan opened the door wide enough to give him some momentum for when he slammed it against Jason's foot. Jason winced in pain and pulled away, giving Devan the opportunity to shut the door before Jason could say anything else.

Shit, this was bad. Who the hell would go to all the trouble to track him down and ask these questions? He played over in his mind everything that had happened between them at the gym, but as far as he knew, no one would have suspected that they were anything more than friends.

Clearly, they hadn't been as careful as he'd assumed.

Matthew was still in his highchair, banging Mr. Fuzzy against his tray. "Baby, I think we're going to have to skip movie morning."

Matthew didn't seem at all concerned.

Instead, Devan grabbed his cell and texted Eli. *I think we might have a problem.*

Eli was in the middle of training with Andrew when Zack came over to the ring. "Hey, I need you for a second."

Andrew glared at Zack, his black hair sweaty from their workout. "This is why you should be in Montreal. Too many interruptions."

Zack threw Andrew a glare of his own. "If this wasn't an emergency, then I wouldn't have interrupted." He then turned his gaze to Eli. "We should talk in my office."

Eli nodded, grabbed a towel, and wiped down. "Give me a few. I'm sure this won't take long."

Instead of the berating from Zack that he'd half expected, he was shocked to see Nolan pacing in the office. "I can't believe this happened."

Eli looked between them. "What's going on?"

Nolan glanced at Zack, who nodded. "You tell him."

"Tell me what?" There was nothing he hated more than being kept in the dark.

Nolan ran his hand through his hair, exposing a light scar along his hairline. "Devan called a few minutes ago. He said he tried your cell but you weren't answering."

"Is he okay? The baby?" Eli's stomach dropped.

Zack reached over and squeezed his shoulder. "They're fine."

"Physically." Nolan sighed. "Devan is a little freaked out, and I can't say that I blame him."

"What. Is. Going. On?"

"Someone showed up at his apartment, wanting to know if you and he were friends or in a relationship. He apparently stuck his foot in the door so Devan couldn't close it."

The concern Eli felt a moment ago was replaced by rage. "What?"

In all the years they'd been together, nothing like this had ever happened to them. He might not have been as big a name back then, but this was insane. "Is he okay?"

Nolan nodded. "He said there are some people hanging around his apartment building though. Mostly across the street, so the building superintendent can't do much."

"I need to go over there."

Zack grabbed his arm before he could take two steps. "And confirm whatever angle these jerks are trying to take? Stupid. One of us can go over."

Nolan shook his head. "No good. If they saw Devan here at the gym, then they know who we are as well. It should be a friend of his."

No, screw this. Eli grabbed the phone from Nolan's desk and called Devan. He didn't wait for him to say hello. "Are you okay?"

"I'm fine. A bit freaked out, but doing okay." Devan's voice shook, which told Eli all he needed to know.

"I want you to take a cab to my mom's house. Bring the few things you need. We can ask Meg or someone else to get the rest of your stuff later."

"I'm not going to run away from this. I have a life. All of Mattie's things are here. I can't send him into confusion because of some bully."

"They're probably Caulfield's crew trying to stir up shit. You'll need to stay somewhere else for a few days, and everything should be fine."

"Eli, I'm not going to give in to this. If I run, then they win."

Surprisingly, Eli didn't give a fuck about winning.

"I know, but if they know who you are, then they're going to continue to harass you." He didn't want to upend their lives, but he wasn't about to let some assholes harass them because of a connection with him. "Let me do this for you. I owe you this at the very least. Let me take care of you properly for once."

He heard Devan swallow. "Fine. I'll take a cab. What's your mom's address again?"

Eli rattled it off. "I need to ditch Andrew, and I'll be right over. Wait a half hour, call the cab, and I should be there waiting."

His mind was already spinning as he hung up, working out the details of what he'd need to do to make sure Devan and Matthew would be comfortable at his mom's house. He'd need to get some groceries, probably pick up some soft blankets for Matthew to rest on. God, he might have to find one of those damned Baby Mozart DVDs. Did he *have* a DVD player?

Zack's chuckle broke his train of thought. "Wow, I've never seen you this focused on something before. Not even in the ring."

"Mom's place isn't remotely babyproofed. I have power tools in the kitchen."

"Just get them there. Then the two of you can figure the rest out." Zack looked out the office window at the ring. "Andrew appears as though he's going to punch something."

"Shit. He's going to be pissed when I cancel the rest of today's training."

Nolan stepped around the desk. "I can take care of him. It might be fun to see if he'll put some of our regulars through their paces."

"I'll do that." Zack kissed Nolan on the forehead. "You stay here in case Devan calls back and needs help."

Eli stopped listening to the two of them making plans. He needed to get to the house before Devan. "I have to go."

And so he did. Without thinking about Andrew, what Stephan would say to him about distractions before the fight, or if someone was watching him here at the gym, Eli marched to the locker room, grabbed his stuff, and left without a backward glance.

He made it to his mom's in record time and was nearly done putting the building supplies and tools away when there was a knock on the front door. He raced over and pulled it open to reveal Devan holding a sleeping Matthew, a giant diaper bag and a folded-up playpen at his feet. Devan's jaw muscle jumped. "I'm furious. But I don't know who at."

"Come in. I'll get the stuff." Eli reached for the bag the moment Devan came in.

Devan had been to his mom's house a few times when they'd been married. It'd been mostly to check in on the tenants, and they hadn't really stayed long. Devan had only met Eli's mom once in the whole time they'd been together. Not because Devan wasn't interested, but because Eli didn't want to subject him to her changing moods due to her dementia. Maybe that had been another mistake on his part, but at the time it had made sense.

Devan looked around the living room, which Eli realized was far too cold for a baby. "I'll turn the thermostat up."

"The place hasn't changed too much."

"The tenants used mom's furniture for the most part. I'll need to get rid of some of it before I rent the place out again." He hefted the heavy diaper bag on his shoulder. "Where do you want to put him?"

"A spare room is fine. He can sleep in the playpen, and I have his toys and books with me. In a pinch, I can use Netflix to entertain him."

It took them a few minutes to get Matthew organized, but thankfully he didn't wake. Devan laid him down, pulled a blanket over him. "He should be good for an hour or so."

They snuck out of the room and went to the kitchen.

Knowing Matthew was in the house, all Eli could see as he looked around were hazards. "This place is a death trap."

"It'll be fine. I'll either hold him or keep him in the playpen for now." Devan rubbed his eyes. "Not quite the relaxing Friday I had hoped for."

Eli went to the fridge, wishing some food had magically appeared while he'd been gone. "I don't have much here. Some chicken, spinach. Stuff for protein shakes."

"I'm fine as long as you have coffee."

Eli hadn't forgotten how much Devan needed caffeine to function. "I'll brew a pot."

Silence filled the space between them as Eli went about his task. No doubt Devan was plotting how to track down whoever had sent the man to his place to read them the riot act. When Eli finished and turned his attention back to Devan, he was surprised to see that he was looking at the wall where Eli had begun repairs the other day.

"Are you putting up pine boards?" Devan looked closer at the patch job. "This will look great with some natural wood. I always found the room to be too dark."

The smell of brewing coffee filled the kitchen, helping Eli relax. "Yeah. Mom never let me do anything around here. She was pretty set in her ways, but I'd always wanted to modernize as much as I could."

"I remember you saying that." Devan turned back in his seat, his brown eyes meeting Eli's. "I wish I'd known her better."

Guilt clawed at Eli's insides. "I wish you'd known her before her strokes. But that woman is gone."

Devan looked away. "What are you going to do now?"

That was becoming a common question for him. "I'm going to go order some groceries and have them delivered. Along with a pizza for you. Then I'm going to call Stephan and fill him in. He'll figure out what's going on and will put a stop to it."

"Do you really think it's Caulfield? Is he trying to out you for more publicity?"

"I wouldn't put it past him." Eli didn't care so much about whether or not people knew he was gay, but Stephan had always stressed that being openly out in the MMA would seriously hurt his chances at furthering his career. "As long as you and the baby are fine, I'm not worried."

"You should be. Eli, this could destroy everything you've worked so hard for." Devan shook his head slowly. "I pushed you when we were together. I wanted to get married and have kids. You never said no, but I realized after you walked away that you were juggling too much: your mom's illness, trying to balance what you needed in your personal life and what you wanted in your professional life. I'm sorry that I forced your hand."

"You didn't." Eli pushed away from the counter and moved to Devan. He squatted down in front of him, and put his hands on Devan's knees. "You did nothing wrong. I . . . When I left, that was all me. My head was . . . messed up and I didn't know how to handle my emotions. I was terrified."

"You wouldn't have needed to handle anything if I hadn't put you in that situation to begin with."

"What are you talking about?"

Devan reached over and rubbed a corner of dried crack fill. "I was angry at you for a long time. You were my own personal villain, which meant you got to shoulder all of the blame. I never had to look at my own actions, what I'd done, because you'd been the one to leave. Since you've come back, I've started to question things. What I did to you."

"You didn't—"

"Yes, I did. Your mom had a major stroke and was living in a nursing home. I should have asked to go with you to see her. Insisted on helping you with that. I'd been so focused on starting my own family that I ignored an entire part of the one I'd already had."

"I could have asked for help. I didn't."

Devan looked up at him, his eyes filled with tears. "You shouldn't have had to. You were my husband."

Eli swallowed past his guilt. "How about we agree that we both made mistakes?"

"Okay." Devan got up and started pacing. "I really fucking hate this. I was starting to feel less than safe in my own home. I don't know who that man was, or what he wanted. They have no right to get involved in my life."

"No one will bother you here. I'll make damn sure of it." Eli stood up and ran his hand through Devan's hair.

"They better not. I don't want to cause you any problems with your career, but if they come after me and Matthew again, then they're going to be sorry."

Eli always knew Devan had a steel core to him, and had always enjoyed when he put it into action. God help the person who tried to hurt his son.

"Why don't you go rest? I'll get some food and anything else you need for the night."

"Yeah. I'll go check on Mattie."

Eli stepped away, not wanting to crowd him. Devan looked out the windows as he passed, no doubt checking to see if there were any lurkers around.

Jesus, what a clusterfuck. When Eli had agreed to come to Toronto to help Zack with the grand opening, the possibility of seeing Devan, let alone dragging him into a public relations nightmare, hadn't been something he'd ever considered. He needed to get this fight done, get the house finished, and sort out whatever this was between him and Devan.

And if it turned out that he was Matthew's biological father, then he'd have another decision to make. For the moment, his focus was groceries and getting a little help.

He pulled out his phone and made a call. "Hey, Max. I need your help."

CHAPTER SIXTEEN

Devan didn't remember drifting off to sleep. One moment he was stretched out on the spare bed, looking at Matthew sleep, and the next he startled awake, the sound of laughter coming from somewhere in the house. Matthew was still asleep, so he quietly tiptoed out of the room and went in search of the voices.

"I know you don't drink when you're training, but here's some wine for Devan. I hope he won't need it this morning, but you never know. And I totally brought junk food because he deserves it."

Devan stepped into the kitchen, surprised to see Max and Grady standing there. "Max!"

While he might not have been as built as Eli, Max was as tall and mostly as handsome. "There he is!" He came over and pulled Devan into a hug. "It's been too long. You never come to the club anymore."

"Do you offer a babysitting service? I would absolutely come if you did. Why are you two here?"

Max laughed. "For you I'd totally add one. Eli told us about your problem. I offered to bring provisions and get anything you needed from your place. I haven't been to the gym in ages, so I'm sure no one watching the place would suspect me."

Relief swept through Devan. "That would be fantastic. There are a few things I didn't think to get when I was rushing out the door."

"Make a list of what you need and write your address down. I'll head over this morning and get what you need. I'll also make sure no one has tried to get into your place."

Eli took Devan by the shoulder. "I need to go back to the gym today. I can't skip out of more training. Not with the match next week."

Devan grabbed a piece of paper and jotted down the things they were going to need. "That's fine. I'll stay here and get organized. I have to work tomorrow, and I'll need to make arrangements for someone to come stay with Matthew." Depending on how Meg and Josh were, he might ask them to look after Matthew. If not, he'd need to take a few sick days and hunker down.

"I have a press conference to attend tomorrow night." Eli clearly wasn't looking forward to it. "It shouldn't be long, because we're not the main event. But with everything that's been stirred up on social media, Stephan said they want us in the spotlight."

"You'll do great." He held out the list, which Grady took and slipped into his pocket.

Max and Grady moved past them. "We'll get out of your hair and get your things. Be back in a few hours."

"Thanks, guys." Devan watched them leave, remembering the time when it used to be him and Eli doing favors for others as a couple.

It wasn't until they were gone that Eli tugged Devan in for a hug. "One more week and all this shit will be done. People will move on to whoever is the next flavor of the week, and your life will go back to normal."

"A *week*?" God, he couldn't put his life on hold for that long. It was going to be a nightmare getting back and forth to work, not to mention needing to make arrangements for the sitter to take Matthew at her house and—

Eli squeezed him hard. "Breathe. You're freaking out."

"Of course I'm freaking out. My life is currently off the rails."

"It's not that bad. I'm here to make sure both you and Matthew are okay. Whatever you need, I'll get for you. All you need to do is breathe. We've got this. Together."

"Okay." Devan gave himself a moment to rest, to relax against Eli's strong body and soak in everything about him. "There's been so much going on, I think my brain is just catching up now."

Eli's fingers brushed the bottom of Devan's hair. "Same. Between you and the fight, it's like I've forgotten why I'd come back to Toronto in the first place."

"What's that?"

"To fix up mom's place and put it back on the market to rent."

Devan tensed and pulled back. "You're not going to stay?"

"I don't know. I want to, but Stephan has my hands tied with my contract. I'll have to talk to him."

Given how much he'd wanted to know about Matthew's paternity, how much time he was spending with his mom, Devan had assumed Eli staying in Toronto was a done deal. He hadn't considered the possibility that Eli wasn't going to be able to stay, no matter what he wanted. "I see."

Eli shook his head. "It's out of my hands."

"I know." God, why had he gotten his hopes up? They both had their own lives, and after three years, he couldn't expect Eli to simply change everything for him. "I better let you get back to the gym. I'll check on Matthew."

"Devan—"

He jerked away, knowing if he didn't leave right the hell now, he was going to cry. "Good luck in the ring." He left without looking back.

Eli's heart hadn't been in his training since the moment he'd stepped into the ring. Andrew's constant berating, not to mention the groin kick he'd landed when Eli wasn't paying attention, hadn't helped matters. Running from training to the house to get Devan set up, their fight—almost fight, disagreement, he didn't know—before racing back to the gym for another session, had taken more out of him than he'd realized.

What Eli really needed was to get something to eat, have a massage, and take a long sit in the steam room. Not necessarily in that order.

Instead he side-stepped another one of Andrew's kicks.

"You can move faster than that." Andrew led with one of the kicking pads, forcing him to defend himself.

Eli bounced around, landing as many hits as he could, despite not being at full power. Today had drained about every ounce of his reserves. Eli tried to land a spin kick and missed.

"What the actual fuck is wrong with you?" Andrew dropped the pads he'd been holding. "Get your fucking head in the fight."

"We've been at this most of today. I'm tired."

Stephan had shown up an hour ago, and had been watching intently from the sideline. "Andrew, take a short break. Let me talk to my boy here and we'll work this out."

Eli climbed out of the ring, grabbing his water as he went. "I'm fine."

"Bullshit. I haven't seen you this bad since your first few matches years ago." Stephan crossed his arms and lowered his voice. "Are you hurt? Do I need to be worried about the fight next week? You collapsing or some shit? That would be worse than Caulfield knocking you out."

"It's fine. You have nothing to worry about." This was the first time in years he'd had to deal with emotional turmoil while training. He'd learn to deal. "Is the press conference tomorrow night all set?"

"Yeah, it'll be good. You're going before the main event guys meet. You've only been allotted twenty minutes, and you'll probably not have to worry about a lot of questions. It's the panel format with the other under-card fighters. Knowing Caulfield, he'll try and cause a stir at some point. Stay your stoic self and it will play great on the sports reports."

The only place Eli wanted to see that asshole was in the ring. "I need to talk to you about something."

Stephan frowned. "Sure."

"Someone has been harassing a friend of mine. Showed up at his apartment asking a whole lot of questions about me."

"What kind of questions?"

While Eli hadn't exactly been hiding his sexuality from Stephan, he hadn't explicitly told him the truth either. "Asking if he was my lover."

Funny enough, Stephan didn't exactly look surprised. "Ah. Is he?"

There was no denying the truth now. "He's my ex-husband."

"So he was the one who used to email you weekly."

Eli didn't know how the hell to respond to that. "Well Caulfield sent someone to cause him problems."

"That wasn't Caulfield." Stephan stepped closer. "That was Jason who showed up. He's an investigator friend of mine who I use to check up on things from time to time. I saw you with him here at the gym, the training sessions, the baby. I needed to know what I was dealing with."

"*What*?"

"I needed to know if this was some new fuckboy I had to deal with. You're starting to get sloppy. If you'd stayed in Montreal like I'd wanted, this wouldn't have been a problem."

Rage flared bright within him. "You asshole. Don't you ever go near them again. Do you hear me? Never again."

"Don't give me a reason to. If it gets out that you're gay, do you know what that will do to your career? All the effort I've put in to make you the rising star that you are will be wasted. Keep him away from the fight, from here. If I get a hint that the two of you are going to make your relationship public, then this will be emailed to Caulfield before the fight."

Stephan pulled out his phone and brought up a picture of Eli and Devan kissing. It was the day that Devan had shown up at the gym, after Devan had put the baby seat into the car. "I'm going to kill you."

"No, you're not. You're going to get your ass back into that ring and you're going to do every little thing Andrew tells you to do. Then you're going to go to the presser tomorrow night and be the fighter the world wants to see. You flat-out deny you're in a relationship if you're asked. If not, if you hint that there's something going on in your personal life, then your ex becomes front and center in the gossip column and your career is over. Do we understand one another?"

The burning rage didn't fade, but Eli didn't know what else he could do but follow Stephan's demands. "This isn't over."

Stephan chuckled. "I'm fairly certain it is. You're locked into a contract with me, so don't think you can dump me and keep going. I'll destroy you."

Eli's stomach bottomed out for a moment. Stephan was right. He'd signed a ten-year contract with him, and at the time, he hadn't realized the importance of some of the fine print that had been added. He'd hoped there would never be a problem and he wouldn't have to worry about getting free.

Stephan reached out and patted Eli's cheek. "Now go train, you beast. You have a fight next week."

Zack wasn't too far away, and sauntered over as soon as Stephan moved back to the ring to speak with Andrew. "What was that about? You look ready to kill someone."

He trusted Zack more than anyone else in the world, but he wasn't about to put another one of his friends into Stephan's crosshairs. "Nothing. I have to get back into the ring."

"I wanted to ask how Devan was doing. Is everything all settled?"

Five minutes earlier, and he would have been able to give Zack an honest answer. "He's fine. Probably deep into an episode of *Dora the Explorer* with Matthew."

For once, Zack didn't notice that Eli was deflecting. "Well, let me know if you need anything else and I'll help."

"Thanks."

Eli crawled back into the ring, knowing that he'd finally be able to unleash his anger on Andrew. "Let's get this shit going."

If Andrew was scared, he didn't show it. "Stephan tells me you've got a little fuckboy on the side. Should have known."

Eli pounced on him. A hook that Andrew wasn't quite able to block followed by a snap kick to the side of his head, before punching him square in the nose. Blood exploded from Andrew's face. "Fuck!"

Eli swiped his feet out from under him, sending Andrew to the mat. He got right in his trainer's face. "If you go near him, if you even talk about him, I'll show you what it means to be on my bad side. You got me?"

Andrew didn't say anything before Eli moved away. Stephan clapped loud enough to draw the attention of some of the other gym goers. "That's what I like to see. The killer instinct that had been missing. Caulfield won't know what hit him."

Shit, he'd played right into Stephan's hands. "I'm hitting the steam room." Before leaving, he tossed his sweat-soaked towel at Andrew. "Too bad about the nose."

He needed to get cleaned up and talk to Devan. Now that he knew the truth of what was going on, they needed to have a united front. Eli didn't want anything else bad to happen.

CHAPTER SEVENTEEN

After Matthew had finally woken up from his nap, Devan moved his playpen to the living room and placed Matthew's toys inside, hoping he could make them both feel at home. Eli had been gone for hours now, far longer than Devan had assumed he would be. He couldn't imagine that he was still at Ringside. While Eli was strong and had crazy endurance in the ring, he couldn't go indefinitely.

Devan had spent the afternoon and evening making sure that the main floor was at least somewhat babyproof. He'd been about to move into the kitchen when there was a knock on the door. Thankfully, this time it wasn't some unknown person, but rather Max, a bag full of items in his arms.

"Oh, thank you so much. Matthew was starting to get fussy, and this stuff will help."

"I didn't know which bag of diapers you needed, so I grabbed what I saw." He handed everything over to Devan. "Oh, and when we were there, a package was delivered to you by courier. I had to sign for it." He handed it over. "I figured you might want it."

The label was from the lab that had done the paternity test. God, this had arrived days earlier than he'd expected. The sudden rush of nerves through him sent his hands shaking. This was the last thing he wanted to deal with today. If Max knew exactly what it was he'd handed Devan, he didn't show it. "Thanks."

"No problem. I'd stay longer, but I have to get over to the bar. We have a new DJ starting tonight, and I don't want to be late in case there's a problem."

The envelope grew heavier every second that he held it. "That's fine. I won't keep you. Eli should be back soon enough."

"I hope I'll see you both at the bar soon." Max shoved his hands into his pockets. "It felt right to see the two of you together earlier."

But Eli couldn't stay in Toronto. And Matthew might be his son. "I'll have to see if he's up for it. It was wonderful to see you again too."

"Okay. Well, take care and call if you need anything else."

"Sure. Thanks again."

Devan watched until Max got into his car, waving and smiling in the hopes that he wouldn't realize how freaked out Devan currently was. He finally closed the door and moved over to the couch. He put the package on the cushion beside him and stared at it.

"Da, da, da." Matthew whimpered, before the smell of a dirty diaper filled the air.

"Yes, baby. I'll clean you up." But he didn't move immediately, unable to take his gaze from the package.

In there was the answer to the question that had been bugging him since he'd first learned of the mix-up. He now had it, and for the life of him, Devan wasn't sure he could bring himself to open the package. No matter what the answer was, the simple act of knowing would change everything.

Matthew started to full-out cry, which jerked Devan from his thoughts. "Okay, let's get you changed and smelling like a rose again."

While he was in the spare room changing Matthew's diaper, he heard the door open and close. Eli had finally come back, which meant that there would be no more putting off the inevitable. "I'm in the room with Matthew," he called. "I'll be out in a few minutes."

Once Matthew was changed, Devan brought him out into the living room. Eli was sitting on the couch where he'd been a short time ago, looking at the package. "It came."

"Max brought it over when he dropped off the rest of my things." He kissed Matthew's temple. "I need to give him a bottle so I can put him down. Then we can talk."

"I'll move the playpen back to the spare room for you." Eli leaned in and gave Matthew a soft kiss to the top of his head, which surprised Devan. "I have something to tell you as well."

It didn't take long for Matthew to get drowsy, and he went to bed easily for once. That left Devan with one final task—to find out what the test results said.

Eli had gotten one of his protein shakes from the fridge while Devan had been out of the room. Eli was no longer looking at the package. No, his gaze landed on Devan the moment he'd emerged from the room. There was no mistaking the look of anger on his face.

Devan slowed his approach. "What's wrong?"

"Sit down." Eli finished his shake and dropped the empty bottle on the floor as he sat down in the chair.

In his experience, nothing good ever followed the phrase *sit down*. He moved past Eli and sat slowly on the couch. "What happened? Did someone show up at the gym? Were they asking questions?"

"No, it's not like that. I know who showed up at your apartment." Eli rubbed the back of his right hand. "It was some investigator named Jason. Stephan sent him there to confirm who you are. He admitted to blocking your communications for years." He sighed and reached for Devan's hand. "He's threatened to tell the public about me . . . us, if I do anything to jeopardize the fight. He'll destroy everything I've worked for."

Devan looked over at him, stunned. "But he's your manager. Why would he do something like this?"

"I think he's worried that I'm going to let my personal life get in the way of business. I'm worth a lot of money to him right now, and I was careless with you. If it gets out that I'm gay, that might ruin my chances of making it to the next level."

"You couldn't have kept a secret like that for the rest of your life," Devan said as he pulled away to cross his arms. "And who says that it'll ruin your chances? Jesus, there are tons of gay men in professional sports. All professional sports. Why the hell is this still an issue anymore?"

Eli shook his head. "It's politics and money. It doesn't matter that people say we'll be treated the same, or that who we sleep with doesn't matter. It still does. And we're not. Maybe someday, but not now."

Devan wanted to go over and hug Eli, but didn't dare. "I'm so sorry."

"Maybe once I get to the big leagues, it won't matter. My skill will keep me there, but it will put a target on my back. Until then, I need Stephan to get me the kind of opportunities I can't get on my own. Not to mention that I still have four years left on my contract with him, then I can look for someone who will accept me for me." He shrugged. "If I do everything right, then he said he'll keep my secret. You and Matthew will be safe."

"God, what the hell is wrong with people?" Devan dropped his face to his hands, suddenly far too exhausted to deal with this shit.

"There's something else. He figures I'll be asked about my personal life. He wants me to deny being in a relationship. Of any kind."

Devan looked up at him through his fingers. "What? You're not going to do that, are you? I mean, you don't have to out yourself, but it's not like you guys are monks. People will assume you get around."

"That's the problem. People will assume, then they'll start to ask questions. He's worried that when they don't turn up any women, it might get people wondering."

"And then they might find out about me." What a nightmare. "What are you going to do?"

Eli sighed and shook his head. "I might not be able to be honest, but I'm not going to deny you either. Fuck Stephan, if I'm asked, I'll say that there's someone special, but I won't discuss it."

He knew Eli was taking a risk saying that much. Devan's heart pounded at the thought.

"Are we going to open that?"

Devan let his gaze fall on the envelope. "I don't know."

"We should. It's here. We both want to know." Eli got up from the chair and moved to sit beside him on the couch. "At least this is something that will make sense."

"I don't know what this is going to do to us. We won't be able to un-know the answer to this." The dam of tears he'd been holding back all day finally broke. "I've tried so hard to give him everything he needs. To be enough."

"Knowing this won't change what you've done for him. You are a great dad. I don't know how you do everything that you manage to do, and still stay sane. Hell, more than sane. You're still fun and funny. Matthew adores you." Eli picked up the package and handed it to Devan. "I know I said that I needed to know, and I desperately do. But I won't force you if you aren't ready. We'll put the envelope somewhere safe until you are. I can wait."

He turned the package over in his hands, picking at the edges. "It would be a shame to have come this far and not open it."

Eli said nothing else, simply watched as he made his decision. Devan looked him in the eyes. "Fuck it." He tore the strip that opened the cardboard and pulled out the documentation.

Plain text surrounded a long chart with numbers and more information than Devan could process. His eye dropped down to the results. His heart stopped for a moment.

"What does it say?" Eli sounded nervous, and Devan wanted to reassure him that everything was okay. But he couldn't quite speak yet. Instead, he handed the letter over to him.

"What does all this mean?" Eli looked up from the form.

"It says that Matthew's DNA is a ninety-nine percent match to me." He swallowed, unsure whether to laugh or cry. "He's my son."

Eli swallowed and nodded. "Good. I'm glad." He folded the paper up and handed it back to Devan. "You should hold on to this. In case you ever need it."

Devan was thrilled to finally know that Matthew was his, truly his, and he wouldn't have to worry about anyone trying to take him away. But, surprisingly, the disappointment on Eli's face caught him off guard. "Are you okay?"

Eli's attention had been locked on to something on the floor. When he looked up, Devan forgot to breathe. He'd only seen that expression once before on Eli's face—the night of Meg's second miscarriage. "I thought he was mine."

Devan pulled him in for a hug. "I'm sorry."

Eli didn't sob, but Devan could feel hot tears soaking into his shirt. "I never wanted kids." But the words sounded hollow.

Devan cupped Eli's face. "You're lying."

"I . . ." Eli swallowed. "When you first said you wanted children, I didn't really think much of it. I never had a dad, never thought I would be able to be one. What the hell did I know about it?"

Devan remembered the first time he'd brought up the topic. They'd both been drinking at a Christmas party and had drunk sex when they'd gotten home. When Eli asked him what he wanted for Christmas, Devan had said he wanted a baby. That had brought a fit of giggles from them both, followed by another round of hot sex. "What changed?"

"I don't know." Eli wiped his face and straightened. "When Meg had the first miscarriage, it hurt. Way more than I assumed it would. I hadn't considered that there might be problems with the pregnancy. Then Mom had another stroke, and it was as though I was losing everything. When Meg miscarried the second time . . ." He gave Devan's hand a squeeze. "I shut down. Thought this was the universe telling me that I was reaching for something that I had no business trying for. I was a fucked-up kid with a mom who was more a child now than parent. I didn't know what to do, to think."

"You shouldn't have run. We could have gotten through this together."

Eli laced their fingers together. "You know Mom was never really that supportive of me being gay. Or of us getting married. Shit, or me being a fighter."

"I know." Devan could count the number of times on one hand that he'd met Eli's mom. She'd been pleasant enough, if a bit withdrawn.

"Growing up, there wasn't a lot of love in this house. I spent more time with Zack and Max at the gym than I did here. Mom loved me, but she had problems of her own. The stroke took away so much of the woman who raised me. She doesn't know who I am anymore. Not really."

Devan knew Eli's life had been hard growing up, but they hadn't really talked much about it. "Why didn't you let me help? I would have come with you to the nursing home."

"You wanted to start a new family, and at first I wanted that too. But the sicker she got, the more everything started to fall apart. I wanted to keep you . . . separate. You were perfect, and I didn't want to taint what we had."

God, they'd both been idiots three years ago. Devan shouldn't have let Eli walk away from him. He hadn't bothered to track him down, show up at whatever gym he'd been training at, and demand an explanation, because he'd been hurt. But this explained everything. Their fights, Eli's withdrawal, Devan's sense that something else had been going on. Eli should have known that he could have talked to him about what was happening. Instead, neither of them had done anything, and their relationship had crumbled. *Complete idiots.*

There was only one way things would ever change. One of them needed to step up and push whatever this was between them in the right direction. Devan set the paternity letter down on the floor, stood up, and tugged on Eli's arm. "Up."

"Where are we going?"

Devan didn't bother to say anything else; it would soon be clear enough. He led Eli up the creaky stairs to the master bedroom. There wasn't a lot in there: the queen-sized bed, a dresser, and one nightstand, all made from old wood. There were building supplies stacked up in a corner, another reminder of Eli's intentions to leave Toronto when the fight was over. Tonight, this moment, might be Devan's last opportunity to prove to Eli once and for all that they could still make their relationship work.

"Dev." Eli stopped moving and turned Devan to face him. "What are you doing?"

"I want to make love to you. Like we used to when everything seemed a whole lot simpler. I don't want to worry about who knows what we do, or who we are to one another. I don't want to worry about your health and you getting hurt more than you are at this fight. I want to feel you on me, in me. I want my husband back."

If Eli had any objections, he didn't voice them. Devan quietly reached for the hem of Eli's shirt and tugged it up until he helped remove it. Yes, they'd had sex on his couch in his apartment, but that'd been more about release and less about this burning need Devan had to reconnect. For the first time in years, Devan touched Eli as though he belonged to him.

Leaning in, he placed a kiss to the center of Eli's chest. The smooth, hairless skin was taut over his muscles. He traced a path with his mouth, across Eli's pecs, over the spot above his heart. Looking up, he made sure Eli was watching as he kissed that spot.

Devan let his hands roam, sliding up Eli's sides, across his rippled abdominal muscles, over his sides to his back. His fingers moved as slowly as Devan could manage, wanting to memorize every dip and valley.

"Dev." Eli reached out and tried to cup Devan's face, but he stopped him.

"No. I get to call the shots. Remember the rules."

"I think we threw the rule book out a long time ago."

Devan cocked an eyebrow. "Maybe, but I'm still in charge."

"Yes, sir."

Devan loved that Eli normally wore jogging pants when he'd been at the gym. They were so much more convenient to pull down, to reach inside, to cup and feel his cock in. He used to tease Eli all the time that way. No matter how long or hard a workout Eli had gone through, he was always up for whatever Devan had in mind. Tonight, despite all they'd been through today, when Devan pushed his hand into Eli's pants and squeezed his cock, he was rock-hard.

"Please tell me you have lube somewhere." He gave Eli another teasing squeeze for good measure.

"Bathroom. In my shaving kit."

"Why don't you get that and a condom and come back here?"

Eli growled but did as he was told. In the few moments that he was gone, Devan unbuttoned his shirt and the front of his jeans. He left the clothing on though, remembering how much Eli loved to strip him.

"That's a sight for sore eyes." Eli had stopped in the doorway, watching.

It was strange that no matter how much he wanted this, would do anything to have Eli again, Devan was surprisingly nervous. "Why don't you come back in? I can't do much to you over there."

"Maybe I was thinking about how I should be the one doing something wonderful to you. You're the one I hurt. I need to make it up to you." Eli closed the distance between them, tossing the condom and lube on the bed before pulling Devan to him and kissing him hard. The passion that had always simmered between them exploded. Devan clutched at Eli's shoulders, his back, tried to pull him as close as he could without climbing inside his body. Eli moved them both forward until the back of Devan's legs hit the bed, sending them both falling.

There was no laughter, none of the silliness that had accompanied their lovemaking in the past. Instead, sighs and moans filled the room.

Eli freed Devan from his clothing, kissing various parts of his body as he moved. His briefs came off with his jeans, exposing his hard, leaking cock to the cool air. Devan sighed when Eli made fast work of the remainder of his clothing before covering Devan's body with his.

Stretched out together—chest to toes—they continued to kiss, to touch and explore. It was a homecoming of sorts for Devan, one that he'd longed for so much over the past few years, he'd started to wonder if this day would ever come.

Eli lowered his mouth to Devan's nipple to tease the tip with his tongue. "I'd forgotten how you tasted. How warm your body gets."

He kissed the side of Devan's neck as he spoke, sending little electric chills through his body. "I've missed you."

Widening his legs, Devan enjoyed the feel of their cocks sliding together. He wanted more than that; he wanted to feel his body stretched around Eli. "Please."

Eli reached for the lube as he continued to kiss and nip at the side of Devan's neck. "I want to do this face to face, but I'm scared I'll hurt you."

"Don't care." Devan couldn't hold back a moan as Eli grabbed his cock with a lube-covered hand. "Please." He widened his legs more.

Eli squirted more lube onto his fingers and carefully stretched Devan's muscles. It had been so very long since anyone had touched him so intimately, Devan was terrified that he would come on the spot. Eli was slow, precise in his movements, starting with one finger, then two, until he was finally able to open Devan up with little effort.

The crinkle of the condom wrapper being torn open set Devan's heart pounding harder. The last man he'd had sex with was Eli, but the changes between the two of them over the past three years made him wonder if they were the same people. Did it matter?

Not to him. He was here with the man he'd always loved, had never stopped loving. For tonight at least, they could both pretend that everything was all right in the world.

Eli positioned the tip of his cock to Devan's hole and slowly pushed in. The burning sensation caused Devan's breath to catch in his throat. He forced his body to relax, to take what Eli was giving him. It took a few minutes, but finally Eli was all the way in and able to slowly thrust in and out of him without it hurting.

Devan moaned when Eli's big hand wrapped around his cock and began to stroke him in rhythm with his thrusts. He fought to keep his eyes open, so he could see every flicker of emotion that crossed Eli's face as they made love.

"I want you to come." Eli increased the tempo of his thrusts. "I want to feel your body squeeze my cock hard. I want to hear you cry out. I want to smell you on my sheets long after you're gone."

His body was burning, racing toward a precipice that he hadn't fallen over with another person in forever. Devan let his eyes slip closed and enjoyed the hot rush of pleasure seeping into every inch of his body. It was too much and he'd been without this touch for too long to keep from coming. His body shook as Eli showed him that he hadn't forgotten exactly how he liked to be touched.

His entire world froze as the first waves of pleasure slammed into him. Devan didn't try to stop his shouts of pleasure as hot come spurted across his stomach. Eli didn't let up, didn't slow down. His thrusts intensified, and he pounded into Devan hard. His roar filled the room, echoed inside Devan's head and reverberated in his body.

Finally, Eli stopped and fell forward to cover Devan once more.

They didn't speak for a while. Eli finally slipped from Devan's body and slid to the side so the entirety of his weight wasn't on him. Devan rolled so his head rested above Eli's heart; the pounding of their hearts eventually slowed, and weariness began to take him over.

"I better get cleaned up." Eli kissed the top of Devan's head.

"M'kay." As long as he didn't have to go anywhere, then he was fine.

Eli moved him over and padded off to the bathroom. Devan was only vaguely aware of the splash of water in the sink and the heavy thud of Eli returning.

"Let me take care of you." Eli manhandled him, wiping come and lube from his body before pulling down the blankets on the bed. "Climb in."

Devan didn't think, didn't worry about what would happen tomorrow. Right then, in that moment, he was going to sleep with the man of his dreams. Within seconds of Eli climbing into bed beside him, Devan drifted off.

CHAPTER EIGHTEEN

For the first time in months, Eli was happy. His body was sore from the battery of intense training he'd undergone over the past month, but mentally he was clearheaded and ready to tackle Caulfield and everything that came after.

His soul was at peace.

This morning, he'd woken up with Devan curled against his side, as though he hadn't been missing from his bed for years. Matthew had woken him up, not with screams or cries, but with an unfamiliar babble. Eli had gotten up as quietly as he could, letting Devan have a chance to sleep in. He'd made an attempt at changing Matthew's diaper—though he ripped one of the little tabs off and had to start over—and fed him his bottle. The simplicity of providing the basic needs of life for another human being touched a part deep inside him. The anger and loneliness were gone as he held Matthew and watched him.

This was what he'd been missing out on since leaving Devan. It was wonderful.

"Shit!"

There was a thump upstairs that had both him and Matthew looking. "I think your daddy is awake."

"Shit, shit, shit." Devan flew down the stairs, his uniform half on. "I have to be at work in an hour."

"Good morning to you too, sexy."

Matthew stuck out his tongue.

"I need to get him changed—"

"Done."

"And fed—"

"Done."

Devan blinked at him. "Wow, this is a new thing for me. Ah, I still have to drop him off at the sitter's. Unless you can watch him today?"

"I can't. I need to get to the gym for a quick workout before I have to prep for the interview tonight."

"That's on TV, right?" Devan blushed. "I've never actually watched one of those things before."

"Yup. It's online as well."

"I'll have to check it out. See if there are any hot MMA fighters on tonight." Devan's eyes sparkled, and Eli couldn't help but laugh.

"Nope, all ugly mugs from getting the crap kicked out of them." He handed Matthew over to Devan. "He's ready to rock. Can I help with anything else?"

Devan stared at him, before breaking out in the most amazing grin. "You've done plenty. I haven't slept that well in months. Thank you."

"It's the least I can do."

Devan gave him a kiss as he took off, grabbing what he needed. "Good luck tonight. I'll be watching!"

With nothing else to do, Eli went to the gym. He limited his training to weights and cardio. He'd been at it for about an hour when Stephan arrived. His hackles immediately went up as he watched him come closer.

"That's what I like to see. My champ working hard. Slept well I hope. We need you looking pretty for the cameras tonight."

"What do you want?"

"Checking up on my investment." Stephan reached out and turned Eli's head to the side, revealing his neck. "A hickey? How old are you?"

"Fuck off."

Stephan let him go. "Lucky for you, people will think it's a bruise."

Eli dropped his weights. "I don't know what I did to piss you off, but you need to back off. I've damn near killed myself for you. Lied about my personal life for years so we could get to this stage. You're the one who's been pushing for this so badly."

"You wanted this career and were willing to do anything to get to the top. Don't pretend otherwise. And you can get down off your high horse while you're at it. You love this every bit as much as I do. You want it, want the applause, probably get off on beating the crap out of someone like Caulfield." Stephan leaned in closer. "Frankly, I don't care who you fuck. You can have a whole house full of boys, and I wouldn't bat an eye. But when your sex life interferes with your ability to win, then I'm going to put an end to it."

Eli had to force his body to relax. "Had you simply let Devan speak to me three years ago, I would have been divorced and probably wouldn't have seen him again. You're blaming us for this, but it's all on you."

Stephan's face went red. "You think you're something special? That the MMA world will never see the likes of another Eli McGovern? You're not. Another cog that we spin up and push into the cage. When you break, I'll simply find another one. I have three more kids as hungry to win, with as much talent, ready to go. The swipe of a pen on a contract, and you'll be replaced. Then what will you do?"

The blood that had been pounding through Eli's body instantly pooled in his stomach.

Stephan nodded. "That's right. Nothing. You'll be a nobody." He moved right into Eli's personal space, until his face was mere inches away. "Stay away from your ex. Because God help you, if you break even a clause of your contract, I'll make your life a living hell. Not only will you never fight again, the stories about you that will hit the media will paint your ex in a not-so-wonderful light. I wonder how long he'll keep his job if there are questions about his character?"

"You can't do that."

Stephan shrugged. "Maybe not. But are you willing to take the chance? Are you willing to see how far I'll go?"

Eli had never once felt intimidated by another man before, but in that moment, he had no doubt that Stephan would live up to what he said.

"Now, I'll leave you to train. We want you at your sternest. I have no doubt Caulfield is going to do everything he can to push your buttons. Verbally, you can chirp at each other all you want, but I don't want you doing anything that will get you suspended."

Eli waited until Stephan was gone before he turned and leaned against the wall. What the hell was he going to do? The fight was too close, and the media attention now too bright. It wasn't as though the fighters had a union to go to for help. He only needed to show up to the interview, answer some questions, and keep his head down until the fight was over. Then he'd see about getting rid of Stephan.

By the time Devan got back to Eli's place, he was exhausted. The blood drive was officially over now, but the number of donors who'd come in during a last-minute push had kept them all hopping. Matthew had been in a good mood at least, babbling away on their way back. Devan had used Eli's car, which had made getting around a bit easier.

The house was empty and far too quiet when he opened the door. This wasn't his home, but he couldn't help thinking it would be a great place to raise a family. There was a small yard in the back, something that they didn't have at the apartment. Not to mention space for when Matthew got old enough to start running around. Places to play and to hide.

Not that he hated his apartment. The thought of having to keep up a house, pay for upkeep while looking after Matthew alone and working full-time? Yeah, that wasn't something he could handle.

"Okay, buddy. Let's get you fed so Daddy can watch Eli on television."

When he found a frozen pasta dish as part of the groceries Max had brought, Devan smiled before tossing it in the oven. It would take a while to heat up, but it was one less thing he'd have to worry about.

The interview was going to be on TSN at seven o'clock, which gave Devan a little time to get changed and ready. Everything had been different from the moment they'd learned that Devan was Matthew's father. Instead of pulling away the way Devan had imagined Eli might, they'd made love in a way that Devan didn't remember ever having done in the past.

His body still tingled at the thought of Eli touching him, holding him. The girls at work had commented on the change in his mood. He wasn't about to admit to them what had happened; too many of his coworkers remembered the fallout of when Eli had walked away.

He kept his joy to himself, along with his secret hopes that maybe there was a chance that Eli would be able to find a way to stay in Toronto after the fight. They could start over, with eyes wide and honesty between them as their number-one priority. Maybe he and Matthew could move into the house here with Eli. Eli could babysit when he wasn't training, and Devan could cover the mortgage, if there was one. It would be perfect.

It might be too much to ask, but Devan was nothing if not optimistic.

Supper wasn't quite finished heating through by the time seven o'clock rolled around, so Devan grabbed a snack to tide him over. Matthew was in his playpen, sucking on Mr. Fuzzy's ear and watching the television.

"Okay, buddy. Time to see Eli in full-on fighter mode. Well, I guess not full-on. I doubt they'll be beating the crap out of one another tonight." At least, he hoped not.

He had the television muted, not caring about most of what was being said. He'd never quite understood the appeal of watching the fights and everything that went on around them, probably because he'd seen the aftereffects of what Eli had gone through.

After the preamble appeared to be over, Devan turned the sound on in time to hear the commentators finishing up.

". . . last week's viral video. The Dragon certainly had some fire in him that night, and we can only imagine it will carry over to Saturday's match."

That damn video again. Maybe if it hadn't gotten so much publicity, Eli wouldn't feel the extra pressure to perform. They showed the clip, grainy and jerky from a cell phone. No doubt the person was moving around to try to get a better angle. Devan couldn't help but cringe half a second before Eli got kicked and fell to the ground. "I don't know how he does that, baby."

Matthew hit Mr. Fuzzy with his toy truck.

"Don't you start getting any ideas. You're my sweet boy, and there'll be no fighting. Ever."

When the video had finished, Eli and Caulfield had taken their seats behind the table, along with a number of other fighters that were a part of the under-card matches. While they weren't the main event, the video had certainly drawn its fair share of interest from the media, with most of the questions seemingly directed at either Eli or Caulfield.

A reporter off camera asked a question. "This is for McGovern. With your fight being a last-minute addition to the ticket, do you feel the effects of not having a long training period will hurt your chances?"

Eli snorted and leaned in close to the mic. "I like my chances as much as I did the first time we met. Hell, I could wipe the floor with him with a broken arm."

Caulfield leaned back in his chair and laughed. "Based on what I've heard you've been doing, you should be worried."

The reporters started asking questions over one another, until Devan was finally able to hear one clearly. "What does he mean? What have you been doing? Have you been trying new training techniques?"

Eli had tensed, his gaze slipping over to someone off stage. "I've been doing repairs on my house and training at the gym. I'm not thinking of opening up a home-repair business, if that's what you mean."

"Home repair. Is that what they're calling it these days?" Caulfield laughed again. "I heard you were busy in the bedroom. Didn't think that meant crack filling the ceiling."

Devan felt as though he were the one getting insulted. Did Caulfield know about him? Eli had said that it was his manager who'd been the one checking up on him, but Caulfield must have also had some suspicions about Eli. Why else bring something like that up?

Shit, was he going to out Eli on television?

Devan's heart pounded, and his appetite vanished. Eli looked pissed off, but Devan knew how to read him better than most. There was fear simmering beneath the surface of his brave exterior.

Eli pushed away from the table, standing up so fast that the fighter sitting beside him barely had time to react. Caulfield must have anticipated the response and reacted in kind, his chair falling to the floor behind him. The speaker who'd been directing questions from the media quickly got between them as Eli and Caulfield glared at one another.

"Keep the hell out of my personal life." Eli bit the words off, as though each one were a verbal punch.

"Scared I'm going to steal your little bit on the side, McGovern?" Caulfield puffed out his chest and flexed his arms. "Maybe show them what a real man is like."

Devan sucked in a breath. "Ah shit."

Matthew banged his toy truck against the side of his playpen.

"Sorry, buddy. I know that's a bad word. But *shit*."

For a moment, Devan was fairly certain Eli was going to beat the crap out of Caulfield right there and then. Instead he reached over the man foolish enough to stand between them and pointed hard at Caulfield.

"I've spent the last month working my ass off so I can kick yours in the ring. There's no one, not now, not ever, who would distract me from that cause. I'm my own man."

"That's not what I heard. You've gone all soft. You're playing with babies."

Eli's face went red. "The only person I've got on my mind is you. You're going down, you ass. And I'll continue to put you down every time you show your meat head anywhere near me."

Caulfield's grin was nasty. "So you're not fucking some hot piece of ass in Toronto? Can't imagine why else you'd be at that shitty gym otherwise."

"I'm single." Eli turned to the camera and leaned over the table. "Hear that, ladies? I'm single, and I'm hot for you. Once I kick this guy's ass, I'll be looking for some fun." And then he winked.

The words might as well have been knives, they cut Devan so deep. Was it this morning that Eli had let him sleep in, changed and fed Matthew as if he were his own? Had they not had sex, made love less than twenty-four hours earlier? Had it only been a few minutes ago that he'd been planning out his life with Eli once again?

God, he was such a fucking idiot.

He knew this was an act. But as much as Devan might dream of the day when Eli could stand up and declare to the world that they were a couple, it wasn't going to happen. It probably never would. Eli was going to have to stay in the closet until the day he walked away from fighting.

That meant years of hiding, of denying who they were. Matthew wouldn't be able to treat Eli like anyone other than Devan's friend. Or, worse, would have to grow up lying about their relationship.

It didn't matter that he cared for Eli; Devan couldn't deny who he was as a person. If Eli's hands were tied, then maybe things weren't going to work out.

The timer went off in the kitchen, telling him that his supper was ready. Without thinking, he turned the rest of the interview off and went to take it out of the oven.

CHAPTER NINETEEN

Eli was emotionally exhausted by the time he got back to the house. Stephan had paraded him around after the press conference was over, arranging some one-on-one time for additional media interviews. Between all of the publicity he was getting and the training he needed to finish before fight day, he wasn't going to have five minutes alone.

At least he knew that at the end of the day, he'd be able to come home and see Devan and Matthew. At least for a little while.

That had been something that he couldn't get out of his mind since Caulfield had called him on it tonight. He'd said he was single, and until a month ago, that had been God's honest truth. He didn't know exactly what was going on between them, didn't know if he was a good enough man, strong enough to be the person Devan and Matthew deserved.

Maybe he was. Maybe being a fighter in the ring had taught him what he needed to know about being a good husband and father, to know when to fight for something, when to concede, when to listen to others and take their advice.

These were all things that he could talk to Devan about once the fight was out of the way. Because as much as he liked to think that he could take on the whole world at once, Eli knew that if he tried, he'd be the one on the mat.

The lights were off when he opened the door. Strange, he'd expected Devan to be up, even if Matthew was asleep. He flicked on the living room lights, and his gaze snapped to Devan sitting on the couch.

"What are you doing here in the dark?"

Devan swallowed but didn't make eye contact. "I saw your interview."

"I couldn't believe how much of an asshole Caulfield was." The entire time he'd been on air, Stephan had been off to the side watching him. You'd think he'd be used to being under a microscope by now, but it still made his skin crawl. "He was trying to get me mad so I'd punch him."

"I'm sure it would have been good for ratings."

Devan sounded as though he'd learned of a family death. "Are you okay?"

"No. I'm really not."

Eli crossed the room and sat down beside him on the couch. "Tell me."

"No."

"Why not?"

"Because I don't want to be one more thing adding stress on you right now." He sighed and finally looked up at Eli. It was clear from his red-rimmed eyes that he'd been crying. "I'll be taking Matthew back to the apartment first thing in the morning."

"What?" Eli pulled back, his hands balling into fists. "Why?"

"I thought I was okay with this, being forced to hide so that it wouldn't hurt your career. I don't want that to happen. But when you said that there was no one in your life . . . I realized that I can't be invisible. I refuse to be."

"What the hell are you talking about?" Invisible? Jesus, he was the furthest thing from that as far as Eli was concerned.

"I think it was the whole 'no one in my life, not now, not ever' part that got me." Devan's laugh was sad. "And then you asked for women to come look you up. Jesus, there's being in the closet, and then there's that bullshit."

Eli remembered the words, how pissed he'd been when he'd said them. "I wasn't about to play his game. I had to go on the attack."

"You made it so we didn't exist. You promised me that you'd say there was someone special. I know you can't be out, but you didn't have to say that you were alone. To make us a lie."

But he hadn't, not really. They might be starting to get back together, but nothing officially had happened. God, they were technically divorced. But Eli hadn't considered how his words would have sounded to Devan, how, given their history, he would have felt. "I'm sorry."

"No, I'm the one who's sorry. I've done it again: tried to force you into a life that you didn't want." Devan got up and looked around the room as though he didn't know where to go. "I'm going to sleep. I'll call Meg tomorrow to come over first thing in the morning with her car to take me back to the apartment."

Every last bit of energy bled from Eli's body. "Don't do this."

"I have to. We're always going to be second in your life. I get it, I do. You've worked hard to get where you are professionally. You have contracts and obligations that you have to live up to." Devan looked away for a moment, swallowing hard. "I have my son. He's what I always wanted in life. A family. Someone to love unconditionally. I can't have that with you and I can't compete with your job. And I don't want you to grow to resent me every time you have to dodge a question about your sexuality."

"I wouldn't."

"You would. You still haven't come to terms with so many things in your life. Sooner or later, we'd start fighting again, and we'd be right back to where we were three years ago. Only this time, Matthew will also suffer. I can't let that happen."

"Dev, please."

Devan shook his head. "Good-bye, Eli."

He went to the spare room and shut the door.

Eli couldn't think, could barely breathe as the cold reality of his situation sunk in. Despite how hard he'd tried, walking this tightrope between his public persona and his personal life, he'd fallen off once more.

His mom had told him once that he was a difficult person to love. That had stuck with him throughout his life, had colored every relationship he'd ever had. Devan was the first person who'd proved his mother wrong. He'd cared about Eli, loved him. And Eli had done everything in his power to push him away.

The light that always sprung to life when he was with Devan snuffed out, leaving him feeling cold. Eli slowly got to his feet and, with one last look toward the spare room, walked upstairs to his empty bedroom.

Devan sat in the front seat of Meg's car and stared out the window. She hadn't questioned why he wanted to be picked up, nor did she pepper him with her normal questions of what had happened. No doubt that would come, but for the time being she was giving him a measure of space.

Matthew had been cranky since he'd gotten up this morning, which hadn't helped Devan's mood. He'd barely slept, instead lying there thinking about Eli on the floor above him. Once again, he had a glimpse of the life he'd wanted with the man that he'd wanted it with, but this time he was the one doing the leaving.

Ironic.

Eli hadn't come downstairs that morning as he was packing up, as Devan had half expected him to. Though he didn't know why he'd hoped for that. It wasn't going to change the fact that Eli was focused on his career, that he would do whatever he needed to in order to become the biggest named fighter he could manage. Devan, no matter how much he wanted to, couldn't compete with something like that.

Meg finally pulled in front of his building. "You take Mattie in, and I'll bring the other stuff for you."

"Thanks."

It was strange coming back to his little home after only being away for a few days. The air smelled of baby powder and laundry. The mess he'd promised himself that he'd clean up was still strewn about his living room. The carpet was covered in stains, and he had no doubt that there were clean dishes waiting to be put away in the dishwasher.

It was his home, and as far as he was concerned, it was damn near perfect.

Despite it missing one key component.

Meg banged the folded playpen as she came out of the elevator. Devan stepped aside, holding the door open for her. "Thanks, hon."

"No problem at all." She looked around the apartment and took her jacket off. "How about I help you get organized before I take off?"

"Josh isn't expecting you?"

"He's gone to work. Plus, I think he knew something was up when you called at seven this morning."

"Sorry, that was a bit early."

Meg waved the comment away. "I'm here for you, no matter the time."

It took about an hour for them to get everything cleaned up and put away. Matthew was content to play for a while before falling asleep once more in his playpen. Being physical, taking the chance to wash and scrub and put away laundry, calmed Devan down considerably. By the time they'd finished and the coffee was ready for them to drink, he knew he was going to be able to keep it together.

Meg must have realized it as well. Once they were seated at the table, she reached over and gave his hand a squeeze. "So, what happened?"

The words spilled from him. The reason for them being chased from his apartment, Eli looking after Matthew, them making love, the interview, every last emotional up and down he'd gone through over the past three days. The tears came at some point, but he let them fall. It felt good to finally get everything out: all the hurt and loneliness, the fact that he still loved Eli and would take him back in a second if he thought things would change.

Devan laughed. "And do you know what's the funniest part?"

"What?"

"We're still married." He got up and went over to the drawer where he'd kept the unsigned divorce papers for so long. The envelope was a weight in his hand. He rolled it up and squeezed it hard before turning back to Meg. "After he signed them, I was ready to drop them off at my lawyer's. I don't know why I didn't. I guess I thought I saw a chance that with him here, with him seeing us and clearly loving Matthew, that we might be able to work through it." He tossed the envelope on the table in front of Meg. "Such an idiot."

"Him or you?" Meg picked it up and looked inside. "Do you want me to take these and drop them off for you?"

"No." It would be so much easier if he let her take charge and never had to think about any of this ever again. "I'll go tomorrow. I need to see this through myself."

It would be the only way he'd ever feel at peace with his decision.

Meg stood up and gave him a hug. "I'm so sorry, hon. I really thought things were different for you two this time."

"So did I." Life had a way of being unfair in the cruelest of ways. He pulled away and did his best impression of a smile. "We'll be fine. Matthew and I will go back to our routine, and I have no doubt Stephan will make sure Eli returns to Montreal so he can keep an eye on him."

"Like everything was before."

Except Devan knew so much had changed in the past month, nothing would ever be the same again.

Meg reached for her purse and jacket. "Okay. I better get back home. I took today off so I could plan a special meal for Josh." She blushed as she spoke.

"Now that sounds like a loaded statement. What exactly do you have planned for Mr. Josh, eh?"

"I took your advice. We had a long, serious conversation about what we both wanted in our relationship, in our family. He was scared, but agreed that he really did want children. He was terrified that I'd miscarry again, and he didn't know how he'd handle that."

"Oh sweetie."

"He loves spending time with Matthew, but saw how hard things have been on you. He was scared he wouldn't be as good a dad as you are. But when we talked about our needs as a couple, not just for now, but also in the future, kids are something that we both want."

Devan chuckled. "The fact that he's holding me as the gold standard terrifies me." He pulled Meg into a hug. "I'm so happy for you. I know the two of you will be amazing parents."

"Thank you. For being my friend and for being so wise. I love you."

"I love you too, hon." He kissed her cheek as he let her go. "And I'm happy that Matthew will have a friend to play with. Oh my God, we can do play dates and go to the movie theatre together on Friday mornings." Devan grinned. "Can you imagine the first few Halloweens and Christmases once they get older? This is going to be a blast."

She laughed. "Well, I have to get pregnant first."

"I have no doubt you and Josh will have a lot of fun working on that particular problem. Far more pleasant than what you did for me."

Meg slipped her coat on before giving his hand one final squeeze. "I didn't see Eli, so I can't say for certain, but from what you told me, it did seem like things were different with him this time. I'm so sorry that it didn't work out for you."

"So am I."

As the door clicked shut and Devan turned to survey his tiny kingdom, he knew that this was his life now, for better or for worse. He was on his own.

== CHAPTER ==
TWENTY

The days blurred together for Eli as the fight drew closer. He found conversations with anyone were annoying at best and painful at worst, so he avoided them as much as possible. Zack had given him a surprisingly wide berth at the gym, as had most of the other members. They all knew about the fight, so no doubt they didn't want to slow down his training.

Andrew had shown up again, his nose purple and one eye black from where Eli had hit him. Neither of them mentioned the injury, or what had led up to it. Instead, Eli pushed himself as hard as he could, beating on Andrew until they were both covered in sweat and his muscles ached from exertion.

Today was fight day, which meant sleep and mental preparation. Warm-ups and lots of stretching to make sure he was as ready to go as possible. He'd arrived at the arena early, needing time to get his head in the game, because currently it wasn't.

All week, every time he stepped foot in the ring, all he could think about was Devan and the look of hurt on his face. He'd been responsible for that look twice now, and both times he'd been selfish in his reasons. At some point he was going to have to come face-to-face with the fact that no matter how much he wanted to be a part of Devan's and Matthew's lives, they were both better off staying as far away from him as possible.

He ran away from mental anguish the same way he ran toward physical confrontation: enthusiastically.

The other fighters made their way into the locker room, increasing the chatter and general noise levels. Andrew and Stephan hadn't arrived yet, giving him the last few minutes of peace before he would have to weigh in and see the referee.

His phone lit up in his locker, a call coming through. Grabbing it, assuming it would be Zack or maybe Max wanting to wish him luck, he was surprised to see a number he didn't recognize coming through. He ignored the call and went back to getting ready. The phone rang again, the same number. God, he didn't need a distraction like this tonight, not with everything on the line. Closing the locker door, he stood up and went to look at himself in the mirror.

While he'd only been seriously training for a month, he was in great shape. His black shorts were simple, but allowed him easy movement in the cage. He'd made sure to shave his head, but left his beard long enough to look good. It was his expected appearance, and God forbid if he didn't give the crowds what they wanted.

"There's my champ." Stephan came into the locker room. "Caulfield isn't going to know what hit him out there tonight. Think you'll be able to take him out in round one?"

"That's the plan." After all the crap Caulfield had stirred up over the past month, he wanted to put him down fast and hard.

His phone rang again in his locker. *Crap, I thought I'd muted that.*

"I've been told that if you win tonight, a clear definitive win, then you're going to be next in line for appearing on a main-card fight." Stephan laughed and slapped him on the back. "What do you think of that, eh?"

"About damn time." He wasn't worried about beating Caulfield, but the news didn't excite him the way that it should have. A shot at a main-card event was what all the sacrifice of the last three years had been about. Now that it was almost in his grasp, Eli couldn't muster up the emotional strength to care.

"That's what I said. You do your part, and I'll make the magic happen on my end." Stephan looked around the room. "You're not the same caliber as the rest of them. You hit harder, faster, and fly around them. You've got great presence in the ring and with the press. It's your time to shine, Eli. Knock this shithead on his ass."

The ref came over then, nodding to Eli. "Time to review the rules and check you out to make sure everything is regulation."

"Yes, sir."

It was standard protocol, and as Eli listened to the rules, nodding where appropriate, his mind wasn't where it should be. He should be thinking about how best to take advantage of Caulfield's weaknesses, how he'd need to wrap him up quickly once he connected with his chin. Instead, all he could think about was the look of devastation on Devan's face when he said that Eli had made him feel invisible. Nothing in the world could be worse than that look.

His phone in the locker rang again, drawing the attention from the ref.

Eli winced. "Sorry. I'll mute it so you can finish."

"Go ahead. We're done here, and everything looks good. I'll see you in the cage." The ref nodded again before leaving the room.

Stephan shook Eli's hand. "I'll head out as well. I know how much you like to be alone before a fight. I'll see you when this is done."

Eli watched them leave, waiting until they'd both left before opening up his locker. The number was the same for all of the calls, and someone had left a voice mail message. Clearly, the issue was urgent. Typing in his password, he heard the last voice in the world that he'd expected—Meg.

"Eli, it's Meg. I'm at Toronto General with Devan and Matthew. There's been an accident. Devan was out walking Matthew in his carriage when a car hit some ice and skidded onto the sidewalk. Matthew somehow got away with only minor injuries, but Devan's in surgery. They won't tell me very much. I know you're supposed to be fighting tonight. But I . . . I thought you should know. I'm going to try calling you again. Just . . . get down here when you can."

The message clicked off and the voice on the other end started talking. "To erase this message, press one. To save it, press—"

Eli turned his phone off.

The blood drained from his head and seemed to pool in his stomach, making him nauseous. His hands shook as he slowly muted his phone and set it on top of his clothing in the locker. With a gentle *click*, he shut the door, then his legs gave out on him. He sat on the bench with a thud, completely unaware of the rest of the world around him.

Devan was in surgery.

He'd been hit by a car.

Matthew had been hurt.

The idea of it didn't make sense, or seem real for that matter. Devan was so full of life, so expressive and enthusiastic about everything. To think of him in an operating room, connected to wires and tubes, a doctor doing God only knew what to him, made his skin crawl. Surgery meant he'd been seriously hurt—internal bleeding, or a horrible bone break, organ issues.

Jesus, he'd been hit by a car.

And there was nothing Eli could do about it.

The other fighters moved around him, and if any of them noticed his grief, they didn't mention it. It wasn't until someone came up and tapped him on the shoulder that Eli mentally came back to his surroundings. It was Andrew, nose still purple and eye still black. "Time to get your hands wrapped."

Eli stood, as though someone had slipped a coin into a toy to get it to move. He held out his hands, but his gaze never went higher than Andrew's stomach.

"What the hell's the matter with you?" Andrew yanked the wrap tight on his left hand. "You look like shit."

"My ex-husband was in a car accident. He's in surgery." The words left him, and he didn't care if he'd outed himself. Devan had always been an important part of his world. He was now in danger.

Andrew froze. "What?"

Eli looked up, knowing tears had welled up in his eyes. "He was walking his son, and a car jumped onto the sidewalk, hitting them. The baby had minor injuries, but Devan is in surgery right now. I don't . . ." He swallowed hard.

He'd always considered himself a fighter, but what he'd accomplished in the ring was nothing compared to what Devan must be going through. He couldn't do this, couldn't be here when Devan and Matthew needed him.

Andrew finished the wrap on his hand before checking his work. "What are you going to do?"

"The fights have started. Our match is third on the card. I . . ." He looked past Andrew to the other fighters who were going through their own preparations. Caulfield was in a different room, no doubt pumped to try to inflict his revenge on Eli.

If Eli won tonight, there'd be another match. Another round of being on the road, doing promotions, and coming back to empty hotel rooms. He'd cut off nearly everything from his life to chase after his dreams. He'd left the care of his ill mother to strangers, and barely took time to check up on her. None of that would change unless he did something about it.

The question was, did he want to?

Only a fool would think this was an either-or situation. Despite the pressure Stephan had put on him to keep things quiet, Eli knew he'd find a way. But every denial he'd be forced to utter would kill Devan a bit more.

Due to forces outside of his control, this *had* become a choice.

Devan or fighting.

He took a step back from Andrew. "I need to leave."

If he was surprised by Eli's revelation, Andrew didn't show it. "It will end your career. Stephan will make sure you'll never fight again. Not to mention the breech of your contract. He'll sue."

"I don't care. Devan and Matthew need me." Eli opened his locker door with a hard slam. "Tell whoever you need to that I'm out."

Andrew nodded. "I'm sorry I called him a fuckboy. I didn't realize it was a serious relationship. I'll let the officials know. You better get out of here before Stephan hears."

Andrew didn't say anything else as he left, letting Eli get dressed. He fumbled with his phone as he pulled on his jogging pants. "Meg?"

"Eli, oh my God."

"How is he?"

"The nurse said he'll probably be in surgery for at least another hour. They said something about needing to put a plate in his leg. They can't tell me much because I'm not next of kin."

"Who is? I can pick them up on the way if they need me to."

"Apparently, you still are. Devan never had that changed." Meg made some shushing sounds. "Matthew is really upset. Wait, you're coming? I thought you had a fight? Is it over?"

"I'm canceling. I'll be there in a half hour. Tops."

He ended the call, slipped on his shoes, and raced out the door.

Devan moaned, unable to fully open his eyes. His brain felt as though someone had opened his skull and poured concrete inside, making the simple act of thinking impossible. He gave up trying and went back to sleep.

Later, he woke up with a full-body shiver. Someone spoke—though he couldn't tell if it was a man or woman—and then his body was enveloped in warmth. It seemed like a terrible idea to waste that blessed heat, so he went back to sleep.

It was a child's song that eventually woke him up.

"Mary had a little lamb, little lamb, little lamb." The voice was familiar, but seemed completely out of place. With great effort, Devan cracked his eyes open. It took a few blinks to clear his vision, then a few more to make sure he was seeing what he thought he was.

Eli was sitting in an orange hospital chair with Matthew on his lap. Singing. "Mary had a little lamb, her fleece was white as snow."

Matthew giggled and stuck out his tongue.

Devan watched the two of them for a few beautiful moments before a wave of pain washed up his body from his leg. "Shit."

Eli's head snapped up. "Devan. Oh God, you're okay. You're awake."

Devan looked over at Matthew and saw that he had a scrape on the top of his forehead and what appeared to be a butterfly bandage on his chin. "Oh, my baby."

"He's okay. The nurse said that it looks worse than it is. Josh took Meg down to Tim Hortons to stretch her legs and get something to eat. I'm sure they'll be back in a few minutes." Eli reached over and pushed Devan's hair from his forehead. "How are you feeling?"

"Like I got hit by a car." It wasn't remotely funny, but he still chuckled. "Ouch."

"That'll teach you to be a smart-ass. Do you remember what happened?"

The events were little more than a blur, and it took a second for his brain to remember. "We weren't far from the apartment. It was dark and cool, but had started snowing. I needed some fresh air and thought Matthew would enjoy the snowflakes. I heard the brakes and reacted. I don't remember much after that." He hadn't had time to get scared. All he could think of was getting Matthew out of the way; his own safety hadn't entered into the equation.

"Whatever you did saved Matthew." Eli leaned over him and placed a kiss to his forehead. "You're one of the toughest, bravest men I know."

Devan blinked again, his brain suddenly playing catch-up. "Wait, you're here. Why are you here? Did you win?"

Eli shifted his hold on Matthew and gingerly sat down on the edge of the bed. "Yes, I'm here. Meg called me as soon as they brought you into the hospital. I was getting ready for the match, so I was a bit later getting to the hospital than I would have liked." He looked Devan right in the eye. "I didn't fight. I left before my match began."

Devan wasn't sure if it was the drugs affecting his hearing, or if maybe he had a concussion that was making him a bit loopy. He tried to sit up, which only served to unleash another wave of pain over him. "You didn't fight? But you've worked for years to get to this point."

Eli looked at him with emotions that Devan couldn't label. "I'll probably be sued for breach of contract as well. But I don't care. That was the worst phone call I'd ever gotten in my life. It took all of three seconds to realize that nothing else matters as much to me as you and Matthew. Nothing."

Meg and Josh came in, a nurse not far behind them. Meg squealed the moment she saw Devan. "Oh my God, you're awake. Oh hon, you scared the shit out of me."

"I'm sure when I have time to process everything, I'm going to be utterly freaked out. But for now, the good drugs are working." Her hug was painful, but Devan wasn't about to stop her. "Thank you."

"For what? I didn't do a thing. And don't worry about Matthew. We'll take him home with us tonight. Keep him as long as you need us to. I want you focused on getting better."

The nurse tapped Meg on the shoulder. "Visiting hours are over soon. He should get some sleep considering all he's been through."

The last thing he wanted was sleep. Devan wanted to talk to Eli, wanted to hold his son and let everything sink in: he was alive and Eli was here with him.

"We'll come check on you tomorrow." Meg took Matthew from Eli as Josh waved to him.

Eli was the last one to leave. With a glance at the nurse, he leaned over and kissed Devan softly on the lips. "I'll see you tomorrow as well."

"Will you?" He shouldn't be so surprised, so hopeful, but he was.

"The minute they'll let me in here." Another kiss and he was gone.

The nurse fussed around him for a few minutes, checking his blood pressure and temperature and adjusting his IV. "How's your pain?"

"It's actually starting to get quite bad."

"I'll check your chart, but you're probably due for some more morphine." She looked over her shoulder toward the door. "Was that your boyfriend?"

Funny that the answer to that particular question was way harder to know now than yesterday. "God, I hope so."

"He's hot."

Devan grinned. "That he certainly is." He grimaced as more pain began to radiate through him.

"I'll get you that morphine."

"Thanks."

As he waited for the nurse to come back, Devan let his mind wander. Eli had left before one of the biggest matches of his career. He'd essentially killed his chances of ever fighting professionally again, or at the very least, made those opportunities far more difficult to obtain.

All for Devan.

He'd been hurt, and Eli had come running without a second thought.

If that didn't tell him what he needed to know about Eli's feelings, Devan didn't know what would. For now, he needed to focus on getting better. If Eli was serious about doing right by him, then he'd be here tomorrow morning. They'd have a chance to talk things out and maybe determine if they might have a future together after all.

CHAPTER TWENTY-ONE

Eli waited in the lobby until it was officially visiting hours, needing some time to collect his thoughts. He'd talked to Meg and Josh last night on their way out. She'd offered to keep Matthew home for a while before coming over for a visit. It would give him time to talk to Devan, to see where they were going to go from here. Despite wanting to have Matthew with him, he needed the chance to talk to Devan alone.

He'd spent most of the morning reviewing press clips and internet posts about his absence from the fight. Caulfield had taken it as a PR golden opportunity, announcing that Eli had been too scared to fight him. Utter bullshit, but unless he made a statement of his own, it was all the media had to go on.

There'd been more than a few missed calls and several texts from Stephan. Each communication had grown more hostile than the last, until Eli had said fuck it and deleted them all. He'd known there was going to be fallout the moment he'd decided to walk away from the fight. For him, the potential legal and professional challenges were nothing compared to the pressure of having to deny who he was as a man. Regardless, his career was something he'd deal with once he had a chance to speak with Devan and knew he was okay.

The moment Eli was able to, he headed for the elevator and went upstairs. Thankfully, Devan had been put into a semiprivate room that didn't currently have another patient. He was sure that wouldn't last long, but for the time being, they had a measure of privacy.

He didn't know exactly how they were going to move forward after this, but Eli knew there was no way he could walk away from Devan again.

The problem was, he didn't know if Devan would want him around.

The hospital floor was far busier this morning than it had been last night. Eli felt like a giant as he squeezed past gurneys and attendants walking in the hall. He heard Devan talking before he made it to the room. Instead of going right in, Eli waited a moment to make sure there wasn't a doctor in there doing an examination.

"I do this all the time, but I'm a crap patient. The girls down at the clinic laugh at me whenever it's my turn to donate blood. I don't mind sticking people, just don't put that thing into me. Ouch!"

"Sorry." The woman certainly didn't sound sorry. "One more vial. And that's it."

"I've used that line before. Totally lies."

"Never. See, you're all done."

"Thank you."

Once the woman and her tiny lab cart left the room, Eli stuck his head around the corner. "Is it safe to come in?"

Devan's face morphed from annoyance to bliss in the blink of an eye. "You came."

"I said I would."

The room was far less oppressive than it had been the night before. A bouquet of flowers had been delivered at some point, which cut some of the antiseptic smell. "Those are nice."

"It came this morning. The girls down at the clinic sent it over."

"Meg said she was going to give them a call."

"The card says to get better soon because they'll miss my sass. I'm not sure how sassy I'll be with a broken leg for the next six to eight weeks and a face that looks like I was beat up, but we'll see."

Eli couldn't help staring at Devan. His face was bruised and scraped from the impact, as were his arms. His leg was in a cast, his plaster-encased foot sticking out from beneath the sheets. "You look like shit."

Devan laughed, but it quickly turned into a grimace. "Thanks. I feel like I've been run over by a car. Oh wait!"

Pulling the chair to the side of the bed, Eli waited a moment before taking Devan's hand. "When I got Meg's message that you'd been hurt, all I could think about was getting to you as quickly as I could. I didn't care about the fight, or myself. I think I outed myself to Andrew."

"You did?" Devan frowned. "How did he take it?"

"I'm sure he knew from before, but it's very different when I'm the one saying it." Slipping his fingers through Devan's, he gave his hand a light squeeze. "I don't care what he thinks. As I sat here last night watching you sleep, I realized that you were right. I had been pushing our relationship to the back burner while we were married. I used fighting as an excuse. With Mom and her strokes, and Meg and her miscarriages, it was as though the universe was telling me that this fairy-tale happiness that everyone talked about wasn't for me. Then I started picking fights with you and . . . I screwed everything up. Stephan gave me an out, and I took it. It was the biggest mistake I'd ever made."

Devan was crying but hadn't said a word.

Eli reached over and tenderly wiped the tears from his cheeks. "This past month, having you and Matthew in my life has opened my eyes to how insulated I'd become. I wasn't a fighter because I was trying to prove something, I was fighting because it was the only time I didn't feel dead inside. That was until I caught a glimpse of what my life could have been. Now, I want nothing else but to be with you and Matthew. To be in Toronto with Mom, to make sure she's okay."

"You're an idiot." Devan's voice cracked. "Why didn't you tell me this before? We could have worked things out."

"I wouldn't have been able to. I didn't know what was wrong. I couldn't admit to myself that the problem was with me and not our relationship."

"I was never sure." Devan rubbed his thumb across the back of Eli's hand. "After you left, I spent a long time trying to figure out if I had pushed you away. I wanted a family so badly that I hadn't let myself admit you may not have wanted the same thing. I knew you'd been working hard trying to make a name for yourself."

"What does fame matter if you're all alone? After three years of going from an empty apartment to an empty hotel room, having every aspect of my life regulated and managed, I realized that this wasn't something that I had my heart in any longer. I missed you."

"I missed you too." Devan smiled. "And I think this goes without saying, but I forgive you for anything you think you've done to hurt me. As long as you promise to do the same for me."

The weight of the guilt that he'd carried for the past three years lessened. "You've done nothing. You're perfect."

Devan snorted, wincing immediately afterward. "Not today I'm not."

"Always." Eli leaned over and kissed Devan's hand above the IV line. "I love you, Dev. I always have."

Tears spilled down Devan's cheeks again. "I love you too." He cringed as he tried to wipe at his face and hit a bruise. "Damn it, you've made me cry."

"Wuss."

They both laughed. Devan looked away, a blush coloring his cheeks. "Since we're laying everything out here, I have a confession for you."

"What's that?"

Devan sighed and began to fiddle with the hem of his blanket. "After you signed the divorce papers, we were in a really good place, so I didn't quite know what to do with them. I didn't want to mail them, so I put them back in my drawer. Then when we fought after the television thing, I assumed that we were officially over. The reason I was out for a walk the other night was to take the divorce papers and drop them in the mail."

Eli nodded. "Meg mentioned as much."

"Wait, she did?"

"Yeah." Eli's chest tightened. "You wouldn't have been out if not for me."

Devan snorted. "If it hadn't been for that, I'm sure there would have been a different reason. But you're missing my point. What I'm trying to say is, I never actually made it to the mailbox. The papers were inside my jacket." Devan smiled slightly. "So technically we're still married."

He sat there and looked at his . . . husband—which was weird to realize—and smiled. "Of course, we're still married."

"If that's not something you want, then I can still send them in. We can start over, or walk away." Devan bit down on his lower lip.

"Is that what you want?" Eli's heart pounded as he hoped that Devan would give him the answer he secretly longed for. "To walk away?"

Devan smiled up at him. "No."

The tension bled from him. "Good. Me either."

"It's probably smart if we take things slowly. Go on a few dates and really see if this is what we both want. I'd want Matthew to be a part of those dates too. If you're going to be around, you need to know what you're getting into. It's not easy raising a child, and you weren't expecting to have one in your life."

Eli had started smiling, his cheeks aching from lack of use. "I like the sound of that. I also have a rule."

"What's that?"

"You were right that I had made you invisible. If we do this, I want to be able to show you and Matthew off. I want to call you my husband and son. Maybe not right away, but someday. I want the world to know that I'm yours and you're mine. I never want you to feel as though you're not important to me, or less important than something else."

He got to his feet and leaned over Devan. Their kiss was soft, and Eli was scared to put any weight on the bed that might cause Devan more pain. Slowly, he ran his tongue across Devan's lips, tasting him as he breathed in his scent. This was what he'd wanted, what had been missing from his life: a feeling of home.

Eli reached up to cup Devan's cheek, which elicited a wince. He pulled back and saw that he'd accidentally brushed up against a large scrape on his cheek. "Sorry."

"We'll have to keep things PG until I'm recovered." Devan patted Eli's chest. "But then I expect to spend as much time in bed as we'll able to get away with."

"Meg is an excellent babysitter." Eli smiled. "And I'll happily pay."

"Oh, you'll pay all right. Do you have any idea the hell she's going to put you through?"

Eli had felt a bit jealous of their relationship when they'd first started dating. They were more brother and sister than anything else. "I promise I'll do whatever I need to re-earn her trust."

Devan smiled. "Good. Well, I guess this means I need to hurry the hell up and get better."

"The doctor said last night that you might need physiotherapy to help regain the strength in your leg. Seeing as I won't be fighting anymore, I can help with that. I'm a pretty good trainer, after all."

The groan that escaped Devan was hilarious. "You're going to kill me."

"No, I won't. I'll give you loving nudges in the right direction." They both laughed, and Eli finally relaxed. "Unless you kick me out, I'm going to spend the whole day with you."

"I think I'd like that."

Together they talked, and Eli knew he'd come home.

═ EPILOGUE ═

There was a surprisingly large group of sports reporters present for the announcement. Devan had worked hard to make sure that he'd be able to use his crutches, rather than have Eli push him in the wheelchair. It was a big thing, given it had only been a month since the accident, but it was important to him to be there as healthy as he could be, as a sign of solidarity.

Eli had been officially dumped as Stephan's client a week and a half ago. There'd been threats of lawsuits—Eli had no business leaving before the fight, it made everyone look bad, blah, blah, blah—but when Eli had been able to prove that Devan was his husband and that his injuries had been considered life-threatening at the time, things quieted down.

He still had the matter of making things right with the public, which was what today was all about.

"Stop fidgeting." Devan tapped the side of Eli's foot with his crutch. "People are going to think you're nervous."

"I am nervous." He jerked his tie until it was nearly undone, which made him look as though he'd been out partying all night. "I have no idea how this is going to go over."

"You can't go out looking like that." Devan got up from the chair Eli had found for him and hopped over. "Come here."

"I feel like I'm choking." Eli's jaw clenched. "I hate ties."

"That's why you're going to work for Zack at the gym. No ties required." He fixed the knot, but before he sat down, he reached behind the tie and loosened Eli's top button. "That will help, and you'll still look good."

Eli looked down at him and smiled. "Thank you."

"You're welcome. I had no intention of letting you go out there looking bad."

"I meant for coming here with me. I don't think I'd be able to go through this alone."

Given what Eli was about to do for him, for them both, there was no way Devan would abandon Eli when he needed him the most. "I'm always here for you."

The stage manager came over to them and gave Eli a little nod. "I'll announce you, then you can come out and make your statement. Are you taking questions?"

Eli nodded. "A few."

"Okay." The man made a note on his paper. "Then let's get this show started."

Devan pulled Eli in for a hug as carefully as he could. "Good luck. I'll be right here for you when you're done."

Eli let out a little huff and walked to the side of the stage.

"Ladies and gentlemen, Eli McGovern is here to make a statement. He'll be taking questions after."

With one final look back at Devan, Eli walked over to the podium. Looking up at the crowd, he fingered the paper he'd set on the podium. "Hello." He cleared his throat and looked down at the speech that they'd worked on the night before. "I'm here today to officially announce my retirement from the MMA circuit."

The reporters rumbled, and the snap and blink of camera flashes exploded briefly.

"Three years ago, I was a happily married man, with my entire career in front of me. I worked hard to get where I wanted to go, and sacrifices had to be made. In my case, that meant me walking away from the one person who loved me more than anything. But what I couldn't be was honest. Not with the world, and not to myself."

Eli paused and glanced over at Devan. Devan wanted to rush out there to Eli's side, to wrap his arms around him, if for no other reason than to show Eli that he wasn't alone in all of this. Instead, he gave him a thumbs-up and a grin.

Eli smiled and turned back to the mic. "You see, the person I was married to was a man. The most wonderful, amazing man I've ever had the privilege of knowing. I made a mistake and walked away from him so I could make fighting my priority. But no longer. The night of my fight with Caulfield, my *husband* was in a serious accident. I had to choose between going to him or fighting. You all know which way I went.

"You can never truly be happy if you can't admit who you are to yourself. It took me three years to realize that. Now that my eyes are opened, I refuse to be in the dark any longer. I'm retiring to spend time with my husband, and I've accepted a new position as trainer at Ringside Gym, here in Toronto."

Eli's shoulders relaxed as he folded up the paper. "Does anyone have any questions?"

The room exploded with shouts.

Eli fielded the inevitable questions about his sexuality, if the league had known and told him to keep quiet, would he ever want to fight professionally again. Devan watched with pride and more than a little awe as Eli patiently and carefully answered each question, never letting anyone get under his skin.

Finally, a female reporter piped up. "How is your husband? What was the accident?"

"He'd been hit by a car while walking his son. The baby is okay, and my husband is well on the way to recovery." He looked over to Devan once more. "I better wrap this up now. I need to get him home so he can rest." And with that said, he turned and walked off the stage.

Right into Devan's open arms. "Oh God, I'm so proud of you."

Eli let out a shuddering sigh. "That was the scariest thing I've ever had to do. In my life."

"You nailed it." He kissed him quickly. "And Grady will be thrilled that you mentioned the gym. He can't say that you haven't been working to build a social media buzz anymore."

"I don't want to think about Grady, or the gym, or anything." He reached over and grabbed Devan's crutches. "Right now, I want to go to the LCBO and grab some wine. Then I want to go back to your apartment, help you pack some boxes, and get you guys moved over to the house."

Devan still couldn't believe that they were going to move into Eli's house. It would take some time, but Devan hoped things would continue to be as amazing as they'd been for the past month. "We can take Matthew over to the nursing home to see your mom. Spending time with her grandson might help her mental state as well."

Eli's smile melted away any lingering doubt Devan had. "She'd love that. And so would I. Come on, let's go home."

Devan let his husband wrap an arm around his shoulders as the two of them stepped out into the light.

Explore more of the *Ringside Romance* series:
riptidepublishing.com/titles/universe/ringside-romance

Dear Reader,

Thank you for reading Christine d'Abo's *Making It*!

We know your time is precious and you have many, many entertainment options, so it means a lot that you've chosen to spend your time reading. We really hope you enjoyed it.

We'd be honored if you'd consider posting a review—good or bad—on sites like **Amazon, Barnes & Noble, Kobo, Goodreads, Twitter, Facebook, Tumblr,** and your blog or website. We'd also be honored if you told your friends and family about this book. Word of mouth is a book's lifeblood!

For more information on upcoming releases, author interviews, blog tours, contests, giveaways, and more, please sign up for our weekly, spam-free newsletter and visit us around the web:

Newsletter: tinyurl.com/RiptideSignup
Twitter: twitter.com/RiptideBooks
Facebook: facebook.com/RiptidePublishing
Goodreads: tinyurl.com/RiptideOnGoodreads
Tumblr: riptidepublishing.tumblr.com

Thank you so much for Reading the Rainbow!

RiptidePublishing.com

ACKNOWLEDGMENTS

Ideas are strange and wonderful things. The idea for *Making It* was the result of a conversation in a car with J.K. Coi, who is always willing to listen to me blather away about my next crazy plot. Thank you, sweetie!

As always, I have to thank my editors Sarah Lyons and May Peterson for their insights and ability to help polish my manuscripts until they shine. A special OMG THANKS to Alex Whitehall, who is the best damn copy editor I've ever had the pleasure to work with. My books shine because of you.

And to my readers, thank you for continuing to visit the Ringside Gym. I hope you'll come back for another round.

ALSO BY
CHRISTINE D'ABO

Ringside Romance series
Working It
Faking It
Losing It (coming soon)

Rebound Remedy

Bounty Hunter series
No Quarter
No Remedy
No Master

Double Shot
A Shot in the Dark
Pulled Long
Calling the Shots
Choose Your Shot: An Interactive Erotic Adventure
Sexcapades
Club Wonderland
30 Days
30 Nights
Submissive Seductions

ABOUT THE AUTHOR

A romance novelist and short story writer, Christine has over forty publications to her name. She loves to exercise and stops writing just long enough to keep her body in motion too. When she's not pretending to be a ninja in her basement, she's most likely spending time with her family and two dogs.

Find Christine online:

Website: christinedabo.com

Twitter: @Christine_dAbo

Facebook: facebook.com/christine.dabo

Newsletter: christinedabo.com/contact.html#newsletter

Enjoy more stories like
Making It
at RiptidePublishing.com!

Patchwork Paradise
ISBN: 978-1-62649-381-0

Until September
ISBN: 978-1-62649-356-8

Earn Bonus Bucks!

Earn 1 Bonus Buck for each dollar you spend. Find out how at
RiptidePublishing.com/news/bonus-bucks.

Win Free Ebooks for a Year!

Pre-order coming soon titles directly through our site and you'll
receive one entry into a drawing for a chance to win free books for
a year! Get the details at RiptidePublishing.com/contests.